Hearts Adrift

A Diver's Romance of Forced Proximity
and Passion
Pebble James

LPS Publishing House LLC

Contents

To the staff and dive community at Scuba Venture of West Lawn, Pennsylvania—

Thank you for opening the door to a world I never imagined I'd find beneath the surface.

Your expertise, encouragement, and genuine passion for diving have transformed not just my skills, but my entire outlook on adventure, connection, and possibility.

Every dive, every lesson, and every story shared has shaped this book in ways big and small.

The camaraderie and professionalism of the Scuba Venture team—and the unforgettable experiences you've given me—brought these characters and this journey to life.

You didn't just teach me how to dive. You reminded me how to breathe deeply, take risks, and chase wonder—on the page and in life.

This story is for you.

Chapter 1

Piper

I step off the plane in The Bahamas, and the heat hits me like a full-body hug I didn't ask for.

Thick, sun-warmed air wraps around my arms and clings to the back of my neck, heavy with salt, jet fuel, and something sweet I can't place it maybe mango, maybe sunscreen, maybe the start of a new life. My sandals slap against the metal stairs as I descend, blinking against the glare bouncing off the tarmac.

I'm sweating before my second foot touches the ground.

My floral maxi dress, cute and breezy in theory, is suddenly a personal sauna. It sticks to my back, clinging to every curve like it's trying to merge with me. The strap of my carry-on digs into my shoulder, and the wind is just strong enough to keep flipping my hair into my lip gloss. I probably look like a hot mess. Emphasis on the mess.

But underneath the discomfort, there's something else.

A thrill. Sharp and electric.

It buzzes in my chest as I follow the crowd toward the tiny airport. My heart's pounding, and not just because the last time I flew solo was to visit my aunt in Toledo. This is different. This is *me*, saying yes to something wild. To adventure. To that

Pinterest board labeled *Escape Plan* I never thought I'd actually use.

And okay, maybe I'm also terrified.

I've only been officially certified to dive for, like, three weeks. I almost chickened out half a dozen times before this trip. And now I'm here, melting in paradise, about to spend ten days underwater with strangers and compressed air tanks and oh God help me the tight wetsuits.

But I booked this trip for a reason. Because something in me needed to change. Still does.

So, I take a deep breath the air salty, floral and foreign I step into the tiny Bahamian airport with my head high and my nerves doing somersaults.

Game on.

The shuttle ride from the airport is bumpy, loud, and somehow perfect. Palm trees blur past the windows, swaying like they're dancing to the beat of the island. The driver hums along to some reggae station, and I press my forehead to the glass, trying to soak it all in. Bright painted houses, wild bougainvillea crawling over fences, kids running barefoot through sunlit puddles.

It's nothing like Chicago.

By the time we pull into the resort there's a cluster of white bungalows wrapped in hibiscus and sunshine. I'm equal parts sweaty, overwhelmed, and buzzing with excitement. Not the fancy all-inclusive kind of place, thank God, but something more real. More personal. Like the kind of place where secrets are kept and found in equal measure.

I don't even wait to drop off my bag.

I spot a weathered wooden sign carved with a sun-faded Sea Pulse Dive Center near the edge of the property and make a bee-line straight for it, heart thudding with something like purpose.

The dive shop is small but alive. A porch with hanging wetsuits sways in the breeze. A rack of BCDs and fins leans half-crooked near the entrance. Someone inside is laughing a big, belly-deep laughter while reggae plays from a speaker set on a high shelf, the bass low and lazy. It smells like neoprene, seawater, and citrus-scented sunscreen.

This is it. This is where the magic happens.

I grip the strap of my carry-on tighter and push the door open, a little bell jangling overhead. Inside, it's chaos in the most beautiful way. Dive logs. Tanks. Maps of reefs marked with handwritten notes. A ceiling fan spins above, doing absolutely nothing to combat the heat.

Behind the counter is a guy with salt-and-pepper hair and skin like worn leather, laughing so hard at something on the radio he wipes a tear from his eye. He glances up as I walk in.

"You must be the new fish," he says, grinning.

I blink. "Excuse me?"

He laughs again. "New diver. Rookie. Fresh out the box."

"Oh," I say, cheeks flushing. "Yeah. That's me."

He sticks out a hand. "Name's Lester. Dive coordinator slash shop genius slash sunburn magnet. You Piper?"

I nod, and his grin widens.

"Cool. Welcome to Sea Pulse. You're signed up for the weeklong adventure dives, yeah?"

"Yeah. I just got here, but I wanted to come straight over. I'm... excited."

He studies me for a beat, and something about his gaze makes me feel like he sees more than he lets on. Like he's already figured out I'm not just here for pretty fish and Instagram selfies.

"Good," he says, handing me a clipboard. "You'll want to sign the usual paperwork. Waivers, releases, the please-don't-sue-us-if-you-panic-and-swallow-half-the-ocean kind of stuff."

I laugh, and just like that, something in my chest loosens.

This place might actually feel like home.

What I don't know yet is that *he* is about to walk in. The storm in human form. My first dive instructor. And the beginning of everything I didn't know I was diving headfirst into.

The door creaks open behind me, and a wave of warm, salt-heavy air rushes in.

I don't turn around at first. I'm still signing the paperwork Lester gave me, pretending to read the part about emergency procedures while secretly wondering if the island sells industrial-strength anti-fog spray for masks.

Then I feel it.

That low, almost imperceptible change in the room. Like the air itself rearranges to make space for someone important. Or dangerous. Or both.

I glance over my shoulder and freeze.

Jorge.

Even from across the room, he radiates heat. Not the kind that burns, but the kind that seeps into your skin and settles deep, like it belongs there. His tank top is worn thin, clinging to a body built from work and water his broad shoulders tapering down to abs that look like they were carved by the tide itself. Ridged and defined like the rippling surface of the sea just before it breaks. Tight. Unforgiving. The kind of stomach that warns you: dive at your own risk.

His skin is sun-warmed bronze, sweat-slicked at the temples. A faint line of salt clings to his jaw, and there's a tattoo winding down his right arm that makes me want to trace it with my fingers—slowly.

And then there are his eyes.

Not just blue. *Deep*. Like reef water at dusk. The kind of blue that makes you hold your breath without realizing why.

He doesn't speak. Doesn't look at me.

But I feel him.

Every step. Every breath. Like a shift in current pulling me somewhere I didn't plan to go.

He disappears into the back room without a glance.

But I'm still standing there, the pen in my hand useless now, my lungs tight with something that feels suspiciously like warning or temptation.

That man is all ocean.

Beautiful. Powerful. And absolutely capable of drowning me.

Before I've even managed to shake off the effect of his disappearing act, the back door swings open again—and Jorge walks in.

Lester grins, clearly enjoying the moment. "Jorge, meet Piper. She's our newest adventurer."

Jorge barely glances at me. His eyes flick over my frame, one fast sweep, and land somewhere in the middle distance like I'm part of the background. His face doesn't move, doesn't soften. Just that same unreadable expression, somewhere between bored and annoyed.

"Certified?" he asks.

His voice is deep and rough-edged, like it's been dragged over sand and seawater too many times. It's the kind of voice that could melt butter—or terrify the unprepared. I feel it drop down my spine, unsettling and electric.

"Yeah," I say, holding up my temporary certification card like a badge, even though my hand is just the tiniest bit unsteady. "Just finished my training back home."

Still no smile. No acknowledgment. He turns to Lester instead, who hands him a clipboard.

"She's signed up for the weeklong reef and open water package," Lester says, tapping the paper. "Some shallow dives, some deeper stuff. Still green, but eager."

I nod like a bobblehead, hoping "eager" doesn't sound as desperate as it feels.

Jorge makes a low sound in his throat. It's not quite an agreement. More like tolerance. "Does she have her own gear?"

I clear my throat. "Just my mask."

His eyes meet mine for half a second. There's no expression in them, just calculation. And then he moves fast, smooth, like a current pulling without warning. He crosses the room to a gear rack, and within seconds he's laying out the essentials on the table with mechanical precision. Wetsuit. Regulator. Buoyancy control device. Tank. Fins.

"This is your setup," he says, voice cool and clipped. "Mask, snorkel, fins, regulator, BCD, tank. Everything here has one job: to keep you breathing and buoyant. If any part of it fails, you'd better know what to do."

He doesn't slow down. Doesn't ask if I'm following. His hands move with practiced confidence, demonstrating where everything connects, how to double-check valves and seals, what to listen for when testing the regulator. It's fast. Efficient. Intimidating.

And the whole time, he barely looks at me.

When I fumble a little with the fin straps, my fingers stiff and clumsy, he pauses just long enough to glance down. His gaze flicks to my hands, then up to my face, sharp and unreadable.

"You ever worn these before?" he asks, voice even.

"Yes," I lie, even though the answer is more like *once, and badly*.

He doesn't correct me. Just keeps moving, like he's already decided I'll figure it out or I won't. His silence feels like its own kind of judgment—worse than yelling, somehow. He's not trying to intimidate me. He just doesn't have time to care whether I'm scared.

When he finishes, he steps back, arms crossed, and gives me a nod so small I almost miss it.

"Boat leaves at eight. Don't be late."

Then he turns and walks out the front door, the bell overhead chiming in his wake.

And just like that, the temperature in the room drops.

I let out a slow breath, only just realizing I'd been holding it.

Lester chuckles from behind the counter, shaking his head. "Don't take it personal. He's like that with everyone. Gruff on the surface, marshmallow underneath."

I raise an eyebrow at him. "You sure about that? He seems more like a sea urchin. Spiky all the way through."

He laughs again. "Give it time. You're not the first to get that look from him."

I glance at the door Jorge disappeared through, my pulse still beating harder than it should be.

Yeah. But I might be the first one who wants to see what's really underneath.

As the door clicks shut behind him, I stay rooted to the spot, my eyes still fixed on the space he left behind like he might suddenly reappear. He won't, obviously. But something about the way he moved how the room changed when he was in it, it lingers like electricity in the air.

I shake my head, trying to focus. Trying to remember why I'm here.

This was supposed to be about *me*. About pushing past my comfort zone, saying yes to the things that scared me, rebuilding my confidence one breath at a time. And yet, here I am, rattled

and flushed over a man who clearly couldn't care less if I existed
or not.

Still.

There's something about him.

Something coiled tight beneath the surface, like he's barely con-
taining the weight of whatever he carries. Something I saw in
the flicker of his eyes when they met mine it was brief, but sharp
enough to make my heart skip. He didn't smile, didn't soften,
but there was a flicker. I'm sure of it.

Maybe.

I feel completely out of my depth, and not just with the gear or
the diving or the unfamiliar heat baking the back of my neck. It's
him. The way he stands, the way he talks absolutely everything
about Jorge is serious, focused, intense. The kind of man who
doesn't waste time on surface-level anything.

And yet, I'm drawn to him.

Not in the easy, flirty, vacation-romance kind of way. This is different. Rougher. Like I've already touched something I wasn't
meant to.

God, I hope he's not my instructor for tomorrow's dive. Or…
worse—*I kind of hope he is.*

By the time I finally make it to my bungalow, the sun is starting
to dip low, casting golden streaks across the porch railing. The
room is small but sweet; cool tile floors, a woven ceiling fan
spinning lazily overhead, and wide wooden shutters that open
to the sound of waves just beyond the palms.

It smells like salt and linen and some kind of tropical flower I can't quite name. It's the kind of place that feels like it should calm you down.

But I'm still buzzing.

I drop my bag on the edge of the bed and sit down beside it, pressing my palms into the mattress like it might ground me. My heart is still ticking a little too fast, and my head's spinning with a hundred small thoughts and gear checks and safety briefings and the fact that I could barely breathe around one very intense, very shirtless dive instructor.

I take a deep breath and lean back, letting my body sink into the softness. The ceiling fan hums above me. Outside, a gull cries out, distant and shrill.

This was supposed to be an escape. An adventure. A chance to find something new inside myself.

And maybe it still is.

But as I stare up at the pale slats overhead, my mind drifts not to the coral reefs or the deep blue sea but to Jorge's voice. His hands. The sharp edge in his gaze.

I can't help but wonder what I've gotten myself into.

Chapter 2

Jorge

T he suns barely cleared the horizon, but the dock's already humming.

Waves slap against the pylons in slow, steady rhythm, the scent of salt and diesel thick in the air. Seagulls squawk overhead, and the dive boat rocks gently against its lines, waiting. I've done this a hundred times, probably more. Pre-dive checks. Guest wrangling. Trying not to lose my patience before we even leave shore.

Then I see her.

Piper.

She's making her way down the dock, and I clock the problem instantly, her fins tucked awkwardly under one arm, mask dangling by the strap, gear bag slipping down her shoulder. The BCD is loose and half-buckled, shoulder straps twisted, and one of the tank bands is flapping free like she didn't even try to secure it. Every few steps, the weight shifts and throws off her balance like she's wearing the gear instead of the other way around.

I bite back a sigh.

Another tourist. Another beginner who thinks diving is just floating with pretty fish and good lighting. They never understand what they're asking the ocean to give them—or take from them.

But still... I watch her.

She's flustered, sure, but she doesn't stop. Doesn't ask for help. Doesn't glance around to see who's judging her even though I *am*. Her face is flushed, strands of hair already sticking to her cheek, and she keeps adjusting her grip like the gear's fighting her every step. But she keeps moving forward, eyes locked on the boat like it's the only thing anchoring her.

Most people like her show up bright-eyed, overly chatty, ready to flirt or ask a hundred questions. She doesn't do any of that. She's quiet. Focused. Determined.

Stubborn.

I know that type. They're either the ones who break down at fifteen feet... or the ones who become lifers.

I shift my weight against the railing, watching her struggle toward me.

I shouldn't care. Shouldn't notice the way her dress from yesterday gave way to leggings and a fitted rash guard this morning, or how she looks good with sun on her skin even flustered, and clearly out of her depth.

But here I am.

Watching.

And already bracing for the headache she's about to become.

Before we even touch the gear, I give her the dive plan.

"Okay," I say, crossing my arms and motioning toward the water off the stern. "This is a shallow reef site the max depth is about twenty feet. No current today. Visibility looks good. We'll do a controlled descent on the mooring line and stay together the entire time. Total dive time is going to be 40 mins."

She nods; eyes wide but focused. Her foot taps lightly against the deck, nerves burning off as motion.

"This is your first open water dive since certification, right?"

"Yeah," she says, biting her bottom lip. "Pool dives and a couple quarry sessions back home. But nothing like this."

Of course not.

"Alright. We'll stay close. You don't need to prove anything. Just breathe slowly, stay neutral, and don't touch anything you're not supposed to—especially the coral."

She gives a little laugh, nervous but trying. "What happens if I do?"

"You'll damage it. Or yourself. And either way, I'll be pissed." I don't smile when I say it, but I'm not trying to scare her, I'm just making her understand that out here, there's no room for ego.

"I'm not here to impress anyone," she says quietly.

That catches me off guard. I nod once. "Good."

I kneel to unzip the gear bag and pull out her setup, motioning for her to join me.

"We'll gear up here, do a full buddy check, and then giant stride entry off the platform. I'll be on your right the whole time. Any problems, signal me immediately. Got it?"

She nods again, firmer this time. "Got it."

And maybe it's just the morning light, or maybe I'm imagining things, but there's something in her face that shifts. Like she's scared but refusing to let the fear win.

I've seen that before.

And usually, it means they're about to fall in love with the ocean.

Or something else.

We're both geared up now, standing on the back deck. Her tank is strapped tight, mask in place, fins on, regulator between her teeth. She glances at me, her expression partly hidden behind the mask, but I can still see it the nerves. The sharp awareness.

I lean in just enough to be heard over the breeze and slosh of water against the hull. "Remember your stride: one hand on your mask and reg, one on your belt or console. Big step out. Let the water catch you."

She nods, swallows hard, then grips her mask and regulator like I showed her. One deep breath. And then—

Splash.

She hits clean, disappears for a second, then pops up with a grin already tugging at her mouth. The mask stayed in place. She's floating high in her BCD, chest rising and falling faster than it should, but she did it. She made it off the boat.

I follow a beat later; one practiced step, a jolt of cool water, and then we're both bobbing on the surface, the boat behind us and the blue stretching out ahead.

She turns toward me, regulator in, eyes wide behind her lenses.

"You good?" I ask, raising my voice just enough to cut through the lapping waves.

She spits the reg and nods. "Yeah. I think so." She's breathless, but not panicked. Just overwhelmed. The way people get when they realize they've finally left solid ground behind.

"Stay close to the mooring line. Follow my lead. You see anything that doesn't feel right, you signal. Got it?"

"Got it," she says. Then, with the kind of bravery I wasn't expecting, she bites down on her regulator, clears her mask, and gives me the OK hand signal...

I return it with the same; thumb and forefinger forming a circle, three fingers up, sharp and clear between us.

And just like that, we descend.

Hand over hand down the mooring line, the surface sliding away above us as the reef rises to meet us below. She moves slowly and carefully, breathing fast but steady. The light fades by degrees, the sound narrows to our bubbles and the subtle shift of pressure in our ears.

We drift along the edge of the reef, just the two of us. She's clumsy. Overcorrects her buoyancy. Fins too hard. Hands moving when they shouldn't. But she listens. Watches me. Adjusts.

And I stay closer than I need to.

I tell myself it's for safety. That I'm monitoring her. But I know better. I never hover like this. I never *watch* like this. Because something about her makes me want to.

Then I spot him.

Benny.

We're about twenty minutes into the dive when I spot him. A green moray eel I see on nearly every dive here. He lives in the same rocky crevice near the brain coral, pokes his head out when he gets curious. I named him a few seasons ago half as a joke, half because he's a fixture on this reef now. Benny the eel. Unimpressed. Unbothered. Harmless.

But Piper doesn't know that.

She sees him slither free of his hideout and jolts. Eyes wide. Her arms twitch out reflexively, and she kicks up, off-balance. Not a full panic, but close. A rush of bubbles spills from her regulator. Her body starts to rise with a burst of air from her lungs, and I know if I don't steady her, she'll pop to the surface without meaning to.

I move fast.

One strong kick and I'm there, grabbing her BCD strap and pulling her into me.

Our bodies collide, close in the water. My hand grips her side. Her chest presses to mine. Regs hissing between us. Her breathing's shallow, fast. Her eyes meet mine, wild and unsure.

So, I hold her gaze.

A long, steady look. Nothing rushed. Nothing loud. Just me and her, suspended in blue. I let her see that I'm not worried. That I'm here. That she's okay. I give her everything I can without words: calm, control, quiet strength. And slowly, her breathing evens out. Her shoulders stop tensing. The panic drains from her eyes like the tide pulling back.

I flash the OK sign.

She hesitates. Then returns it. Her hand is shaking.

Benny slips back into his crevice like he's bored with the whole show.

But I don't move.

Because this isn't just a routine safety grab.

Not anymore.

She recovers slowly.

Not all at once. Her breathing steadies in small increments, her body relaxing in degrees. I stay nearby as she resets, letting the water carry her weight while she finds her rhythm again.

I drift back beside her, give her space, but I'm still close. We continue the dive.

Twenty more minutes beneath the surface. Her buoyancy improves. Her finning smooths out. She starts moving with the ocean, not against it.

And I watch her.

She pauses beside a sponge, following a pair of angelfish with that same wide-eyed wonder I haven't seen in a long time. She's not afraid now. Just amazed.

And I'm not watching the reef anymore.

I'm watching *her*.

Because something about Piper Morgan is pulling me in deeper than I should go.

And I don't know if I'm going to swim away from it or let myself drown.

Chapter 3

Piper

B ack on the boat, I can't tell what I'm feeling more if it's relieved to be breathing fresh air or completely humiliated.

My first real dive and I practically freaked out over an eel. An eel that, apparently, Jorge knows by name. He wrote it on a slate underwater right after pulling me back down—Benny, in bold block letters, like it was the most normal thing in the world. Like it's some kind of reef pet and I was the only one who didn't get the memo.

I peel off my mask and push my hair back, the salt already drying on my skin. My chest is still tight, not from fear anymore, but from the memory of how close he was. His body against mine, the firm grip on my BCD, the way his eyes locked onto mine until everything else disappeared.

I should be embarrassed.

And I am.

But there's something else, too. A low, charged flutter in my stomach that has nothing to do with fear and everything to do with Jorge.

He hasn't said much since we surfaced. Just helped me out of the water, unbuckled my gear with those same quiet, efficient hands, and then stepped away like nothing happened. Like he didn't just hold me underwater while I tried not to melt inside my wetsuit.

I sit on the bench, wrapping my towel tightly around my shoulders like a shield, and stare at the sea.

Out of the corner of my eye, I feel him watching me. When I glance up, our eyes meet just briefly, but fully. Like a jolt.

It's not polite or casual. It's focused. Intense. Like he's still down there with me, reading my pulse through the water.

I look away first, heat rushing to my cheeks, my heart thudding loud and fast in my chest. I can still feel the pressure of his hand on my side, the solid weight of his presence. And that look?

That look makes it very, very hard to breathe.

I came here to get away. To find something I lost in the noise of my real life.

Instead, I found him.

And I have no idea what I'm doing.

But just as I'm trying to convince myself to forget about it; to chalk the whole thing up to nerves and nitrogen he walks by, pauses, and leans down close enough that I can smell the salt on his skin.

"Drink with me after your first dive," he says, voice low, unreadable. "Local bar. Nothing fancy."

Then he walks away.

And I just sit there, blinking, towel clutched to my chest, heart doing something wild and dangerous.

He wants to have a drink with me.

And not in a group setting. Not with the other divers or Lester cracking jokes in the background. Just him and me.

He said it like it was nothing. Like it was practical. Like asking someone to rinse a wetsuit or check a tank valve. But it didn't feel like nothing. It felt like everything. Like a door cracking open to something I wasn't sure I was ready for but deeply, deeply wanted.

I sit there wrapped in my towel, heart thudding, lips parted like I might say something if he turned back around.

He doesn't.

And I can't stop smiling.

I can't believe my luck.

Chapter 4

Jorge

I'm surprised I invited her.

I usually avoid getting involved with the tourists. They come and go, here for the photos and the fantasy, maybe a quick fling if the mood and cocktails are right. It's cleaner to keep my distance. Easier. Fewer complications that way.

But there was something about the way she looked at me after the dive like she was uncertain, flushed and wrapped in that towel like she didn't know whether to hide or exhale. And yeah, I'd already crossed a line by pulling her into me underwater, but that was instinct. This was something else.

Intentional.

I didn't even think it through. Just passed by, paused, and the words were out of my mouth before I could pull them back.

"Drink with me after your first dive."

The second I said it; she blinked up at me like I'd offered her a map to a secret.

Now I'm standing near the back of the boat, rinsing gear, trying to convince myself it was nothing. A casual offer. Just two adults sharing a drink. No expectations. No story behind it.

But my pulse is saying otherwise.

I glance at her out of the corner of my eye. She's still sitting where I left her, towel clutched like armor, staring out at the water like it's going to explain what just happened.

I've made a mistake.

Or maybe I haven't.

I guess we'll find out soon enough.

The local bar is already buzzing by the time I get there. It's tucked off the main road, half open to the breeze, the walls strung with old fishing nets and photos of tourists who came and went. There's a band setting up in the corner, strumming soft chords on a beat-up guitar, and the air smells like grilled pineapple and something stronger poured over ice.

And then I spot her.

Piper.

She's sitting at the bar, back to the door, chatting with the bartender like they've known each other for years. Her hair's down, tumbling in damp waves over her shoulders, and she's got a drink in her hand that glows pink under the lights. She laughs at something the bartender says, head tipping back just slightly, and that sound cuts right through the noise in the room.

She looks nothing like the girl I pulled out of a panic twenty feet underwater.

She looks confident. Relaxed. Like this place fits her in a way the dive boat didn't.

I walk toward her before I talk myself out of it.

She turns, catches sight of me, and her face changes. Softens. That same smile from the boat, but warmer now, like she wasn't sure I'd actually show up.

"Hey," she says, voice easy, like we do this all the time.

I take the seat beside her.

"You settle in alright?" I ask.

She nods, lifting her drink. "Rum punch. Possibly lethal. Want one?"

I shake my head. "I'm good. For now."

She watches me over the rim of her glass, and for a second, we just sit there, breathing in the quiet weight of what this is—whatever this is.

And for the first time in a long time, I don't want to be anywhere else.

She sets her drink down, turns slightly toward me, and asks, "So what's it really like living here? Not the tourist version. The real one."

I don't answer right away.

Most people want the brochure story the endless sunsets and coconut cocktails. But she watches me like she wants more. Like she'd actually listen.

So I tell her.

About the island. About growing up here. About the hurricane that took out half the marina when I was nineteen, and the dive mentor who taught me everything I know. About the reef we just dove, and how it's changed over the years. The good and the bad.

I don't usually share this stuff. Not with visitors. Not with anyone, really.

But with her, it doesn't feel like oversharing.

It just feels easy.

I catch myself staring at her, drawn to her vibrant energy and genuine curiosity.

She tilts her head, a soft smile playing at her lips. "What?"

I shake my head slowly, a low chuckle escaping me as I glance away briefly, embarrassed at being caught. "Nothing. It's just you ask good questions. Most people don't really care about this stuff."

Piper's expression softens further, and she leans in just a little, close enough now that I notice the faint freckles across her nose. "Well, I'm not most people."

"No," I agree quietly, holding her gaze. "You're definitely not."

The space between us feels smaller now, charged with an electric current that's both dangerous and tempting. Her eyes linger on mine, as though she's silently daring me to close the distance.

"Can I confess something?" Her voice is quieter now, almost a whisper.

I lean in instinctively, matching her tone. "Go ahead."

"Earlier, underwater... when you grabbed me? I thought I'd panic more, but instead—" She pauses, biting her lower lip like she's weighing whether to continue.

"Instead?" I prompt gently, pulse hammering in my chest.

"Instead," she breathes, leaning in so our shoulders almost touch, "it made me feel safe. Grounded. And maybe a little brave."

The honesty in her voice catches me off guard, pulls at something deep inside my chest. I exhale slowly; the sound lost beneath the soft strumming of the guitar. "Good," I say finally, the admission coming easier than expected. "Because that's exactly how I wanted you to feel."

Our eyes hold, the rest of the bar fading away until it's just her and me in this suspended moment, one that feels fragile and potent all at once.

Then, abruptly, the moment shatters.

Jack's rough, amused voice cuts through the intimacy as he saunters toward us, a beer dangling loosely in his hand. "Well, look at this. Jorge finally stepping out from behind the dive counter."

Piper sits up straighter, her smile faltering slightly as she glances between me and Jack, curiosity flickering in her expression.

My jaw tightens instinctively. "Jack," I warn softly.

Jack ignores my tone, grinning at Piper. "You must be something special. This guy never lets anyone close—especially not tourists." He nudges me playfully. "Careful, Jorge, or she'll have you believing in love at first dive."

I bristle at the teasing, possessiveness surprising me with its intensity. My tone sharpens, more defensive than I'd intended. "Don't you have a boat to prep or nets to untangle?"

Jack chuckles, raising his hands in mock surrender, backing away with amusement still clear on his face. "Alright, I see how it is. I'll leave you two alone, for now."

He disappears back into the crowd, leaving Piper and me wrapped in sudden, awkward silence.

"Sorry," I mutter, feeling strangely exposed. "Jack's got no filter."

Piper's lips quirk again; her eyes curious. "He seems to think there's something between us."

My pulse quickens; words caught in my throat. But before I can respond, Jack's voice rises again across the bar, louder this time, carrying urgency:

"Jorge! You better get out here—fast."

I turn sharply toward his voice, instantly alert. "What's going on?"

Jack's face has gone serious, eyes shadowed with genuine concern. "Your boat," he says grimly. "It's taking on water."

Piper's eyes widen, her hand unconsciously brushing my arm as I stand abruptly.

"Go," she whispers quickly. "I'll be fine."

I hesitate only a second longer, the weight of our unfinished conversation heavy between us, before turning and racing after Jack into the night, heart pounding with more than just concern for my boat.

Chapter 5

Piper

I hesitate outside the dive shop, my sandals sinking slightly into the warm sand as anxiety knots my stomach. Through the open doorway, I see other divers already gathered, chatting easily as they gear up. After yesterday's shaky start underwater, I'm not exactly eager for another round of embarrassment.

"Good morning, sunshine!"

I jump, turning quickly at the playful greeting. Lester, the resort's relentlessly cheerful concierge, strides toward me wearing a blindingly bright floral shirt and his usual carefree grin. His dark curls bounce as he approaches, eyes sparkling with amusement.

Despite myself, I smile. Lester has that effect. "Morning, Lester."

His brows lift in mock concern. "That's not your usual sunshine smile. You look more like someone heading in for a root canal than a dive lesson. What's got you so serious?"

I laugh quietly, tugging nervously at the frayed hem of my T-shirt. "Just nerves, I guess. Yesterday wasn't exactly my finest moment underwater."

He tilts his head knowingly, leaning closer with exaggerated secrecy. "Want to know a little insider info about Jorge?"

"Definitely," I say, my curiosity outweighing my embarrassment.

"Jorge may look like a grump, but under all those scowls, he's a big softy. And—" he drops his voice, eyes gleaming, "he's impressed by courage. You showed a lot of that yesterday."

"You really think so?"

Lester's playful expression softens. "I know so. And between us? I saw how he looked at you last night at the bar."

Heat floods my cheeks. I duck my head, trying not to grin. "He probably looks at everyone that way."

"Oh, no." Lester chuckles. "Jorge barely looks at anyone. Especially not like that. Trust me it's a good sign. So chin up, sunshine. You've already done the hardest part."

I laugh under my breath. "What, surviving your fashion choices?"

He gasps, clutching his chest in mock offense. "This shirt is vintage, thank you very much. Straight out of the 'What Not to Wear' archives."

"You mean the 'Please Avert Your Eyes' collection?"

"Exactly," he says, beaming. "My fashion causes spontaneous laughter. It's a public service."

His over-the-top confidence makes me laugh harder, the tension in my shoulders finally easing.

"Seriously though," he adds, more gently, "you've got this, Piper. And hey, if Jorge gives you any grief today, just imagine him slipping on deck in flippers. Works every time."

"Noted." I grin. "Thanks, Lester. I needed that."

He gently nudges my shoulder, guiding me toward the shop entrance. "Anytime. Now get in there, show Jorge and yourself what you can do."

As Lester heads off toward the lobby, whistling cheerfully, I straighten my shoulders and step inside the dive shop. For the first time this morning, I'm actually feeling hopeful.

The dive shop is alive with chatter and movement as I step inside, carrying Lester's earlier encouragement like a shield against my lingering anxiety. Behind the counter, Lester settles effortlessly into his domain, his bright floral shirt matching his cheerful mood.

"All right, dive crew!" Lester announces warmly, waving a dramatic arm toward me. "Our newest diver, Piper, has officially arrived."

Everyone turns toward me at once, their gazes curious, assessing. I give a shy wave, hoping my smile looks steadier than it feels.

A tall, athletic man dressed in a sleek, designer wetsuit steps forward first, offering a practiced handshake. His grin is confident, slightly arrogant. "Hey there, Piper—I'm Chuck. And this," he says, nodding toward the woman beside him, "is Laura, my fiancée."

Laura, elegant and coolly composed, gives me a polite smile that doesn't quite reach her eyes. Her blonde hair gleams under the shop's fluorescent lights, and designer sunglasses rest casually atop her head. "Nice to meet you," she says evenly, clearly sizing me up with a single glance.

"You too," I respond softly, feeling distinctly out of my element.

"Don't mind them," says a shorter, exuberant man, practically skipping over to shake my hand. His curly brown hair seems to bounce along with him, matching his boundless enthusiasm. "I'm Rahn. Yesterday's dive was amazing, wasn't it? I bet today's going to be even better. Absolutely nothing can go wrong."

His enthusiasm is infectious, drawing a genuine smile from me. "I hope you're right."

Chuck crosses his arms, raising an eyebrow skeptically. "Famous last words."

Rahn leans dramatically against the counter, rolling his eyes with theatrical exaggeration. "Ignoring Chuck optimism is the only way to dive."

Lester laughs softly, shaking his head at their playful banter. I relax a little, grateful for Rahn's sunny outlook.

Across the shop, a smooth, confident voice cuts effortlessly through the noise. "Optimism is fine but experience beats optimism every time."

We all glance over at the speaker. He's a lean, dark-haired man standing apart from everyone else, meticulously inspecting his dive gear. He glances up, eyes calm but faintly amused, clearly comfortable being the center of attention.

"That's Matt," Lester whispers theatrically from behind the counter. "Our resident solo diver. He prefers the company of fish to us mere mortals."

Matt's lips twitch into a small smirk, hearing Lester's comment. His gaze settles on me, quietly appraising. "Welcome, Piper. Stick close enough and you might pick up something useful."

I blink, caught between admiration and irritation at his casual arrogance, but I manage a polite nod. "Good to meet you, Matt."

He inclines his head, already returning his attention to his regulator, clearly done with the conversation.

Before I can process anything more, the back door swings open and Jorge steps into the shop, instantly drawing everyone's focus. My pulse skips at the quiet intensity of his presence. His eyes meet mine first, holding briefly, softer than they were yesterday. The faint warmth there makes my stomach flutter.

"All right, everyone," Jorge announces, his voice firm but noticeably gentler today. "Gear up, we head out in five."

The group disperses, moving toward their gear. I approach the racks, reaching for my tank and BCD, bracing myself for the awkward heaviness from yesterday—but today, the equipment feels lighter, manageable, almost natural.

Lester notices, flashing me an approving thumbs-up from behind the counter. "See, sunshine? I told you—you've got this."

For the first time, as I tighten my straps and stand tall beneath the weight, I think I actually might.

Thirty minutes later, we're skimming across the water, the sun high overhead, sparkling off glimpses of moving waves. Jorge stands at the helm, confident and focused, the wind tugging at his shirt. I sit near the rail with Rahn, who's practically vibrating with excitement.

"Tiger Beach, baby!" he says, throwing both arms in the air. "I've been dreaming about this since I booked the trip."

Rahn, already halfway into his wetsuit, nearly topples over with excitement. "This is going to be epic! Bring on the sharks!"

Chuck snorts from across the deck. "Let's hope your dreams didn't include being lunch."

"I'm too fast to be lunch," Rahn replies. "Also, I'm stringy. Bad texture."

Matt stands silently off to the side, calmly adjusting his gear with practiced ease. He glances over at Rahn's enthusiasm, shaking his head slightly, clearly unimpressed.

Lester leans over from the captain's chair, grinning. "Relax, everyone. The sharks here are locals. They don't bite unless provoked—like Matt when someone touches his gear."

Matt doesn't look up. "Keep talking, Lester. See what happens."

Everyone laughs, the tension breaking just enough to let nerves breathe.

Jorge cuts the engine. The boat drifts into stillness. He turns, his voice calm but commanding. "Tiger Beach is home to reef and lemon sharks. They're curious, not aggressive. Stay calm. Stay close. And remember—they sense fear and flailing."

"Guess I'm dead," Rahn mutters.

"You'll be fine," I say, smiling.

He grins at me. "Thanks, dive buddy."

Jorge's eyes meet mine briefly, and something unspoken passes between us.

"All right. Buddy checks. Get to it."

As the group finishes gearing up, I wrestle awkwardly with my wetsuit. Somehow, the neoprene feels stickier today, resisting every movement. I tug and hop clumsily, losing balance briefly and stumbling into a pile of fins stacked nearby.

"Easy there, sunshine!" Lester calls playfully from the captain's chair, giving me an amused thumbs-up. "One leg at a time."

Heat rushes to my cheeks as Chuck chuckles under his breath. Rahn shoots me an encouraging smile, offering a thumbs-up of his own. "You've got this, Piper! Gravity's overrated anyway."

I laugh despite my embarrassment, finally managing to zip the wetsuit closed with a frustrated grunt.

Jorge steps closer, his voice gentle but teasing, just loud enough for me to hear. "You need help next time, just ask. The gear won't bite."

I glance up, startled by the warmth in his eyes. "Promise?"

His mouth curves faintly, voice dropping lower. "Promise."

My heart quickens at his closeness, but before I can respond, Jorge straightens, returning to his instructor's voice. "Okay, everyone, buddy-check your gear. We're descending to about thirty feet. Stay calm, stay close, and remember the sharks prefer confidence."

As we slip into the water, anxiety and excitement swirl through me. I catch Jorge's reassuring nod just before I lower myself below the surface.

This time, when the ocean envelops me, I welcome it—ready for whatever awaits below.

The underwater world is breathtaking, sunlight filtering softly through the turquoise waters as I carefully adjust my buoyancy, finally finding some confidence. Around us, reef sharks glide gracefully, their sleek bodies effortlessly slicing through the current, mesmerizing in their quiet power.

I'm so absorbed watching them that I don't notice the tangled safety line floating loosely around my fins until Jorge gently taps my shoulder, startling me slightly. He gestures calmly, motioning toward the mess I've made.

Heat flares in my cheeks, embarrassment flooding me as I nod quickly. Jorge moves closer, patiently reaching to help me untangle the line.

Our hands brush beneath the water, and despite the wetsuit barrier, a jolt of electricity surges straight through me. I glance up sharply, heart racing, certain I've imagined it but Jorge's eyes hold mine steadily, his expression shifting from calm professionalism to something deeper. Something warmer.

This definitely isn't my imagination.

Before either of us can react further, the atmosphere around us changes abruptly. Jorge's eyes widen slightly, his attention snapping upward. Instinctively, I follow his gaze and freeze.

A massive tiger shark, easily ten feet long, passes silently overhead, gliding with an eerie grace just inches above us. Its sheer size and undeniable presence make my breath catch sharply in my throat.

I look quickly to Jorge, my heart hammering in my chest but the calm in his gaze steadies me instantly. He reaches out, gently gripping my wrist, anchoring me as the shark moves past, utterly indifferent to our presence.

As the giant disappears gracefully into the depths of blue, Jorge and I remain locked together, suspended in silence, the intensity of the moment vibrating between us.

He squeezes my wrist softly, a gesture of comfort and reassurance, but something more lingers in his touch. Our eyes hold again, the ocean around us forgotten for one fragile heartbeat.

Then, reluctantly, he releases me, signaling gently to move forward with the dive.

But even as we continue on, my pulse refuses to slow, echoing the quiet truth beneath the waves.

Whatever just happened down here—I know it wasn't just me.

As the dive draws to an end, Jorge checks his dive computer, signaling clearly that it's time to ascend. I nod in response, my heart still fluttering from both the encounter with the tiger shark and the unexpected intensity between us.

We slowly rise, the turquoise ocean around us growing brighter. At fifteen feet, Jorge calmly signals for our safety stop. Hovering side by side for three quiet minutes, every second feels stretched, charged by his closeness and the lingering awe of the dive.

Finally, Jorge checks his dive computer one last time and gives me a thumbs-up to surface.

Breaking through the surface, I pull out my regulator, inhaling deeply, savoring the fresh, warm air. Jorge surfaces beside me, removing his regulator and pushing dark hair away from his face, droplets glittering in the sun as they trail along his neck.

"You good?" he asks softly, eyes gentle yet searching mine.

"Better than good," I reply breathlessly. "That shark was…"

"Incredible," he finishes for me, a genuine smile tugging at his lips. "You did great."

Warmth rushes through me at his praise, but the quiet intimacy of the moment is quickly interrupted by Rahn's enthusiastic voice breaking through the water nearby.

"Oh my god! That shark was huge! Did everyone see that?" Rahn practically bounces as he surfaces, laughing joyously. "Best day ever!"

Chuck surfaces right after, shaking his head and dramatically exhaling. "I thought it was headed straight for Rahn. I figured we'd finally see him stop smiling."

Laura surfaces beside Chuck, pulling off her mask with practiced elegance, smirking. "I don't think anything can stop Rahn from smiling."

Matt emerges from the water next, utterly calm and collected, as if surfacing from a leisurely swim rather than a shark dive. Removing his regulator, he fixes Rahn with a mildly exasperated look. "Less flailing next time. Sharks appreciate composure."

Rahn grins unapologetically, splashing lightly in Matt's direction. "Optimism and sharks mix just fine, Matt!"

Matt just shakes his head slightly, an amused yet dismissive smile tugging at his lips as he swims gracefully toward the boat ladder.

Above us, Lester leans eagerly over the railing, waving cheerfully. "Glad you all survived! No shark snacks today!"

I laugh softly, swimming toward the boat ladder where Lester extends his hand, helping me smoothly onto the deck. Jorge follows closely behind, his powerful presence unmistakable as water slides down his wetsuit, glinting in the sun.

Lester leans closer as I remove my gear, whispering playfully, "See, sunshine? Told you today would be incredible."

My gaze shifts briefly to Jorge, who's quietly climbing aboard, his eyes subtly finding mine as if pulled by gravity. "You were definitely right," I whisper back, smiling warmly.

Lester chuckles knowingly before returning to the helm, leaving me standing quietly on deck, surrounded by the chatter of Rahn's excitement, Chuck's dramatics, Laura's amused laughter, and Matt's aloof calm.

But even amidst all the noise, it's Jorge's quiet, steady gaze that I feel most vividly—anchoring me in a way I'm only beginning to understand.

As the boat glides steadily toward the dock, conversation drifts around me like soft background noise, voices mingling with the gentle hum of the engine. I lean against the rail, half out of my wetsuit, but my thoughts are miles away completely consumed by Jorge.

Every subtle glance toward the helm sends heat surging beneath my skin, my pulse quickening each time our eyes briefly connect. He's standing confidently at the wheel, water still glistening on his tanned skin, the damp fabric of his wetsuit outlining every hard line of muscle. It's impossible to look away.

My breathing becomes shallow, heartbeat pounding faster, and suddenly, I'm acutely aware of a different warmth pooling between my thighs an intimate, distracting wetness that has nothing to do with our dive. I shift restlessly, squeezing my thighs together, my body responding to thoughts I shouldn't be entertaining.

This isn't just vacation infatuation; this feels deeper, more reckless. Jorge is off-limits, my instructor, responsible for all of us.

Yet boundaries seem increasingly blurry, overshadowed by the memory of his hands brushing mine underwater, sending jolts of desire through my veins.

"Piper? Hello—anyone home?" Rahn's voice breaks into my thoughts, playful but insistent. "Did you even hear me?"

I blink quickly, cheeks heating as if Rahn can read every thought flashing through my mind. "Sorry, I drifted. What were you saying?"

"Just telling Matt here that sharks absolutely do smile," Rahn says proudly, gesturing toward Matt, who's sitting quietly nearby, calmly coiling a safety line.

Matt lifts one eyebrow, mildly amused but clearly unimpressed. "Sure they do, Rahn. If that helps you sleep tonight."

Chuck snickers from across the boat, nudging Laura lightly. "I'd side with Matt on this one. Sharks smiling sounds like wishful thinking."

Laura chuckles softly, shaking her head affectionately. "Come on, let Rahn dream a little."

Matt just shrugs, a faint smirk tugging at his lips. "Dream all you want, just don't wave at them next time. It's embarrassing."

Their laughter blends with the gentle rush of waves against the hull, but I'm barely paying attention. My focus slides helplessly back to Jorge, my body still pulsing with an undeniable ache as I watch him steer us gracefully toward the dock.

Lester steps beside me, voice gently teasing. "You doing okay there, sunshine? You look pretty lost in thought."

I force a quick smile; grateful he can't see the intensity of my internal battle. "Yeah, just thinking about...everything."

Lester chuckles knowingly, casting a subtle glance toward Jorge. "Some dives do that to you."

He has no idea how right he is.

As the boat eases gently against the dock, Jorge's eyes flick toward me again, lingering just long enough to make my pulse spike once more. I release a shaky breath, realizing with startling clarity that I'm definitely in trouble and yet, part of me can't wait to dive even deeper.

After docking, the others drift toward the resort, leaving Jorge and me alone at the rinsing station, quietly preparing our gear for tomorrow's dive. The late-afternoon sun casts golden warmth across the dock, intensifying the quiet, charged energy between us.

"You seemed comfortable down there today," Jorge says casually, breaking the silence as he rinses off his regulator. He flicks a glance toward me, eyes warm yet carefully guarded. "Feeling better about diving?"

"Definitely," I reply softly, hanging up my wetsuit. "Though I think it's less about diving itself and more about who's guiding me."

His mouth curves into a faint, amused smile, his gaze lingering on me for a thoughtful moment. "Just part of the job. You're the one doing the real work."

I reach casually toward my fins, deliberately letting my fingertips brush softly along his arm. The contact is brief but sparks something intense beneath my skin.

"Speaking of your job," I say lightly, keeping my voice innocently playful, "you wouldn't happen to know someone who could show me the real island—the stuff tourists usually miss, would you?"

He pauses, eyes sharpening with intrigue as he meets my gaze fully. A slow, knowing smile spreads across his lips. "I might. Are you asking?"

I tilt my head slightly, holding his gaze, pulse fluttering. "Maybe. Depends if you'd consider helping."

He chuckles quietly, eyes deepening with interest, voice dipping into something softer. "Careful—I might say yes."

"I'm hoping you will," I murmur softly, letting my eyes linger just long enough to let him know I mean it, before stepping slowly away.

As I walk toward the resort, my heart pounds triumphantly, each confident step feeling as though I've just hooked something rare and exhilarating, something only I know I've caught.

Chapter 6

Jorge

The sun's nearly gone, just a fading glow bleeding into the horizon, leaving the sky stained in dusky purples and molten gold. The dock beneath my boots creaks gently as it settles into the stillness of early evening. The air's thick with salt and the soft scent of sun-warmed wood, and I should feel calm. This time of day is usually when the island exhales when everything slows, breathes, resets.

But I don't feel reset. I feel strung out, restless. Like something inside me won't settle no matter how still the water gets.

I haven't been able to stop thinking about her since the moment she walked away from me on this dock.

You wouldn't happen to know someone who could show me the real island...

Her voice replays in my head with maddening clarity—soft, teasing, full of layered meaning. It wasn't a question. It was an invitation with edges, delicate but deliberate. It's been circling me all damn day, and every time I think I've shaken it, it slips right back in.

I lean against one of the dock pilings, rubbing the back of my neck, jaw tight. I've heard plenty of lines from tourists over the years their flirty, bold and clumsy. Piper's wasn't any of those. It was quieter. Smoother. She didn't even have to try. That's what makes it dangerous.

And the way she looked at me when she said it like she already knew the answer.

I exhale hard through my nose, trying to dislodge the memory, but it rushes in sharper instead.

The rinsing station. Her wetsuit half-peeled down, clinging to her hips. Damp curls falling around her flushed face. The water dripping down the side of her neck, catching in the hollow above her collarbone. She didn't even realize what she was doing to me, standing there so relaxed, so comfortable in her skin. Or maybe she did.

When her fingers brushed mine even just a fleeting, incidental touch my whole body would go still. Like my nerves were suddenly wired wrong. I'd already been on edge all day, but that moment? That moment lit something up in me I've been trying to bury for years.

I should've pulled back. I should've said something neutral and walked away.

Instead, I lingered. I wanted more.

Which is exactly the problem.

Because Piper isn't just a tourist. She's this kind of tourist; the kind that asks questions with her eyes, listens with her full attention, and says things that make you want to hand over pieces of yourself before you even realize you're doing it.

And I can't afford to hand over anything.

Not again.

The sun has all but disappeared now, leaving behind a slow, fading warmth in the air and a violet haze where the sky meets the sea. The dock creaks beneath my feet as I pace, the soft wood bending gently with each step, and the water around me is still unnaturally so. It mirrors everything with such precision it almost feels staged. The kind of calm that should bring peace, but tonight, it only sharpens the noise in my head.

I've tried to shake her. All day I've told myself I'd move past it, that the memory of her voice would lose its grip. But Piper's words have been circling me like a current I can't swim out of, quiet and unrelenting. I keep hearing that teasing lilt in her voice, watching the way she looked at me as if she already knew I wouldn't be able to stay away. And maybe I did too, the second she smiled at me like that.

It isn't just what she said. It's how she carries herself, like she's only half-aware of the way she draws people in. Or maybe she knows exactly what she's doing. She stood at the rinsing station earlier with her wetsuit half-peeled down, her hair wet and curling around her face, and I couldn't stop watching the way the droplets slid along the curve of her neck. She didn't posture. She didn't try. She was just... comfortable. And present. And impossible to ignore.

I told myself I wasn't going to get involved. That this would be another week, another guest, another goodbye. But nothing about this feels like that. She doesn't feel temporary, even though I know she is.

The pressure in my chest has been building all afternoon, rising like a tide I can't control, and I know from experience there's only one place I can go when my head starts spinning like this.

So, I turn toward the dive shop, crossing the dock without thinking, my mind already shifting into gear. The familiar smell of neoprene, salt, and worn rubber greets me as I step inside, the shadows wrapping around me like an old routine. I leave the lights off—there's no need. I know this space like I know the back of my hand.

Moving quietly through the shop, I begin gathering my gear. The motions are automatic, comforting in their precision. I check the straps on my BCD, run my fingers along the seams of my fins, listen to the steady hiss of the tank as I test the pressure. Regulator. Weights. Mask. Every piece in its place. Every step is a ritual. There's a rhythm to it, something steady and grounding that pushes back against the chaos spinning inside me.

Here, in this space, nothing is complicated. There's no room for second-guessing underwater. No space for emotion. Just breathe. Buoyancy. Balance. Control.

It's the control I need most of all.

Because the way she looked at me today—the way she touched my arm like it was nothing, like it didn't send a ripple of heat straight through me that has had me on edge ever since. And I know myself well enough to recognize what's happening. The weight of wanting her is settling in my bones, dangerous and slow-burning.

I need the silence of the ocean. The pressure. The distance from the surface and everything that comes with it.

I'm not diving to escape her.

I'm diving because it's the only way I can keep myself from doing what I'm not supposed to want.

By the time I step out of the dive shop and onto the dock, my gear feels like an extension of my body. The weight across my shoulders is grounding, the regulator clipped neatly to my chest, everything in place. I've done this a hundred times when I would slip into the night and into the water when I needed it to be quiet, the noise in my head. But tonight, the noise is stubborn. It's not fading. It's sharpening.

Then I see her.

And for a few long, still seconds, I forget to breathe.

Piper is standing near the edge of the dock, her back to me, silhouetted in the soft, silver haze of moonlight that glides across the water. She's not moving. Just... there. Like she belongs to this place in a way that makes no sense and perfect sense all at once. Like she's part of the tide, the sky, the stillness.

Her hair is loose, damp at the ends from the humidity, soft waves curling over her bare shoulders. The breeze toys with it, lifting a few strands, tucking them behind her ear, and I watch the motion like it's sacred. Her profile is partially turned but enough for me to catch the line of her jaw, the delicate slope of her nose, the subtle curve of her neck as she tilts her head slightly toward the sea.

She's wearing a simple tank top with faded cotton that clings just enough to show the shape of her, and shorts that leave her legs bare, tan and strong and kissed by the sun in a way that tells me she's been out living in the world, not hiding from it. Her calves are toned, feet bare on the planks, and there's something raw and real about that detail that makes my chest tighten.

There's a tension in the way she holds herself but not fear, not nerves. Waiting. Or maybe thinking. Like something's turning over inside her, something she hasn't shared with anyone else. I've seen that expression in divers before a descent the quiet bracing, the mental shift. But this isn't that. This is something else. Something that feels like it belongs to me, though I have no right to it.

She's beautiful. Not just in the obvious way though *God,* she is but in the way she *exists*. Like she doesn't apologize for the space she takes up. Like she was built for this dock, for this night, for the moon to pour itself over her skin.

And then there's the rest of her. The part I've been trying not to let in all day. The way she listens not just to words, but to silences. The way she sees things most people overlook. Her curiosity, her ease, that stubborn, sunlit kindness she carries even when she's teasing me like she's got my number and knows exactly what to do with it.

And I think I know—I'm already gone.

I haven't touched her beyond that brief graze of her fingers against mine, but she's *in* me now. Under my skin. In my blood. In every part of me that used to feel unreachable.

I grip the shoulder strap of my gear tighter, standing there like an idiot, completely rooted in place. She hasn't seen me yet. But I see her. All of her.

And she's not just standing there under the moonlight.

She's wrecking me.

I take a step down the dock, then another, and the sound of my boots against the worn planks blends with the soft hush of water beneath us. I move slowly, like getting too close too fast might shatter the stillness between us.

She doesn't turn around, but I know she hears me. Her posture shifts only slightly. The tilt of her head, the loosening of her shoulders. She knew I was coming. She was waiting.

When I reach her side, I pause. Close enough to feel the warmth coming off her skin. Close enough to catch the faint, lingering scent of salt and sun and something unmistakably her. My voice is low when I speak it's barely more than breath.

"You're out late."

She turns to me slowly, like she's unfolding from some private thought. Her gaze lifts to meet mine, eyes soft but direct. The moonlight cuts across her features, carving silver along her cheekbones, catching in her lashes. She doesn't smile. She doesn't need to.

"Couldn't sleep," she says. Her voice is quiet, like mine. Careful. Like she knows this moment matters, but she's not going to push it too far. "Too quiet."

We fall into silence again. A long one.

But it's not empty.

It's thick with things neither of us wants to say aloud. Questions. Warnings. Heat. Curiosity. The tension between us crackles softly, held in place by restraint and something more dangerous beneath it. We're toeing the edge of something we both feel but aren't ready to name.

She glances down, then back up at me. Her eyes flick toward the gear slung across my shoulder, and I see the shift in her expression before the words even come.

"Can I come with you?"

Her voice is steady, but there's something underneath it, something that makes my pulse press harder against my throat. It's not the question itself that unravels me. It's the way she says it. The way it's not about the dive at all.

I don't answer right away. I let the silence stretch, watching her. Feeling her. The moonlight. The water. The weight of my own resistance collapsing one quiet piece at a time.

She doesn't fill the silence. She just waits.

That's what gets me.

I drop my gaze to her lips for half a second—less. Then back to her eyes. And everything in me settles. Not with certainty. Not with control.

With surrender.

"Yeah," I say quietly. "You can."

I don't explain. I don't qualify it. I just let it sit between us.

And when she exhales so soft, relieved, like she wasn't sure I'd say yes it punches through something in my chest I didn't even realize I'd been bracing against.

We don't move right away. We just stand there, the two of us, wrapped in moonlight and salt air, saying more in silence than words ever could.

And deep down, I know—this is the moment I let her in.

Chapter 7

Piper

The ocean at night carries a stillness that feels almost sacred, like slipping into someone else's dream. The surface gleams faintly under the moonlight, a gentle shimmer rippling across the waves, but as we descend, that light disappears quickly, swallowed whole by the dark. It isn't frightening exactly, but it's disorienting at first like losing the horizon, losing the sky. The edges of the world fall away, and all that's left is breath, movement, and the soft hum of water surrounding me like a second skin.

Everything is quieter. Slower. Muted. Creatures that scatter during the day emerge from shadowed crevices, an octopus unfurling itself from coral, its limbs shifting through color as it glides silently by. A school of tiny fish swirls like smoke just outside the narrow cone of Jorge's flashlight, their bodies flashing with silver before disappearing again into the dark. The reef feels more alive than it did in daylight, but also somehow more fragile, more secretive. Like it's showing us something it doesn't share with everyone.

I stay close to Jorge, watching the way he moves ahead of me with that quiet certainty that belongs only to people who know the ocean as home. His fins cut effortlessly through the water, his shoulders steady beneath the beam of my light. Every so often, he looks back at me, and the connection is instant, just a nod, a glance, the soft sweep of his hand signaling me to follow.

There's no sound but the soft roar of my breath in my ears, and yet I feel more communicated with, more understood, than I have on dry land in days.

I realize then how deeply I trust him, not just to keep me safe, but to *see* me. Even here, in this strange, suspended world where I should be unsure of everything, I feel grounded. I feel held.

I don't think it's just the dive.

There's something about the way he's attuned to the space around him, the way he moves like every motion is considered, like everything he does has purpose. My eyes keep drifting toward the lines of his body, the way his muscles shift with each controlled movement, the way his hands are strong and precise hover just beneath his light as if guiding it with instinct rather than thought. It's not just beautiful. It's magnetic.

Beneath the surface, in the dark, I don't feel lost.

I feel like I'm right where I'm supposed to be.

And maybe that has less to do with the water than it does with the man leading me through it.

Down here, time doesn't move the same. It stretches, slows, folds in on itself. There's no sound but the steady rhythm of my breath, the muted rush of water in my ears. The world narrows to the pulse of the ocean around me and the man just ahead, lit only by the narrow glow of our dive lights.

Jorge swims a little slower now, not because he's uncertain but because he doesn't have to perform. There's no audience here, no eager divers to instruct, no checklist to run through. Just him, and me, and the slow, living hush of the reef at night.

And maybe it's the darkness, or the way light flickers across his face every time he turns, but something about him feels different here. Lighter, in some strange way. Unarmored.

He's still strong, still steady, still built like someone who could shoulder the weight of anything without flinching. But in this moment, in this space, there's a quiet in him that feels rare. Sacred, even. His body moves with intention but not effort, like the ocean recognizes him as one of its own. There's no tension in his shoulders now, no clipped edges in his movements, just flow. Ease. Stillness wrapped around strength.

And yet, somehow, it makes him feel more human than ever. Not less intimidating, just more reachable.

He hovers near a coral head, adjusting his light to follow the soft movement of a nocturnal sea cucumber inching over the rock. He doesn't call my attention to it. Doesn't make a show of pointing it out. He just watches, head slightly tilted, quiet curiosity written in the line of his jaw, the slow, deliberate patience of his breath.

I stay back a little, watching him more than the reef, drawn not just to the sight of him but to the *feel* of him in this space. The way he belongs here, without needing to take up space. The way he's present without being performative. Everything about him feels quieter under the water, but not less intense. If anything, it's the opposite. He feels distilled here and reduced to essence.

When he turns to check on me, our lights catch each other's masks, and for a second, all I can see is his eyes. Deep, dark, and unreadable but somehow entirely *there*. They find mine and hold, not probing, not pulling, just... steady. Like the eye of a storm that hasn't chosen a direction yet.

Something in my chest contracts—sharp and slow. The current between us deepens, stretches thin across the space of a few feet and far more than that. There's no way to smile in a dive mask, but I think he sees mine in my eyes. His light dips slightly. Just a flick of movement. But it feels like something was said.

And then he turns back toward the reef, continuing on like nothing happened.

But something *did*.

And it's still unraveling inside me.

Down here, we don't speak. We can't. But that doesn't mean we're silent.

Jorge signals a slow turn with two fingers, his beam sweeping forward like a gentle invitation. I follow, mimicking the gesture with a nod, adjusting my direction without hesitation. The water shifts around us, cool and full of soundless motion, but I don't feel lost in it. I feel synced to him like we're moving through the same rhythm, some quiet current that's more than just training.

He pauses ahead, lifts his light, and flashes it upward in a short pulse. A check. I recognize it instantly and it meant to check my air status. I glance at my pressure gauge, then raise my hand and make the "OK" sign, circling my thumb and forefinger slowly, steadily.

He turns his head toward me, meeting my eyes through the mask, and for the briefest second, he doesn't respond. He just looks at me—really looks.

Then he gives the signal back.

One hand, thumb and finger forming that same familiar shape. But the gesture feels... heavier somehow. Not because he doubts me. But because he sees something. Because maybe he's trying to say something with it that has nothing to do with my oxygen levels at all.

The current moves gently between us, and we hover there for a moment, suspended in shared stillness. His light catches in the water, glowing faintly between us like a tether. Our eyes hold, masks fogging slightly at the edges, and something pulses through me it's not adrenaline, not nerves. Something warmer. Steadier. Something that feels like understanding.

We're only a few feet apart. Not touching. Not speaking. But the space between us feels full.

Every time his hand moves, every time our lights cross, it's more than safety checks and guidance. It's language. A dialogue I feel in my chest more than I understand in my mind.

He turns away first, slowly leading us forward, but I feel the echo of that moment following me;settling somewhere low and deep, where words wouldn't have reached anyway.

We break the surface slowly, as if neither of us wants to leave the quiet below. The night air touches my face like a whisper, cool against my damp skin. My lungs expand fully for the first time in what feels like hours, and I let my breath ease out in a long, steady stream, careful, controlled.

I reach up, gently clear my regulator, and let it hang loose at my chest. Jorge does the same beside me. The boat isn't far, maybe twenty feet but we both stay still.

Suspended.

The sky above us is endless, dark velvet stretched with stars, and the water is so calm it reflects them almost perfectly. For a moment, I'm not sure which direction is up. It's disorienting and beautiful, like the dive never really ended.

We float side by side in the soft pull of the tide, bodies rising and falling in the same quiet rhythm. My mask is still in place, droplets sliding down the lenses, blurring the edges of the world—but I can see him clearly. Jorge. Steady, quiet, the moonlight touching his face in a way that softens him. His breathing is slow, practiced. Familiar. But there's something different in the set of his shoulders now. Something quieter. Unmasked, even if we both still wear them.

He's not looking at me. He's watching the open water, or maybe nothing at all, but I can feel him. Not just physically, not just as a presence beside me, but in that invisible space that connects two people when something shifts between them and neither of them wants to be the first to say it.

I drift a little closer. Not intentionally, but not by accident either. My foot brushes his for just a second, and I don't pull away.

He doesn't either.

It's quiet. Not just the kind of quiet that fills the spaces between words but the kind that means something. A charged kind of stillness that feels more like a conversation than anything we could say aloud right now.

He finally turns his head toward me, slow and deliberate, and our eyes meet through the fogged lenses of our masks. We don't smile. We don't nod. But something flickers between us in that glance—recognition, maybe. Or understanding. Or surrender.

I don't know how long we will stay there.

But eventually, he shifts, gives a small, subtle signal toward the boat. I nod, wordless, and follow.

As we begin the slow swim back, the silence stays with us, draped between our bodies like a current we're both caught in.

Something changed down there, something neither of us can name yet.

And I know, the second I set foot on the boat, I won't be able to keep it inside any longer.

The boat sways beneath us in a slow, lulling rhythm, the sound of water brushing against the hull rising and falling like a breath held just below the surface. Our gear clinks softly as we shed it piece by piece, the silence between us thick and strangely comforting, like we've both agreed without words—that the night doesn't need to be filled with anything but this shared quiet.

Jorge moves beside me, focused as always, unbuckling straps and coiling hoses with that quiet confidence that's so distinctly his. The glow from the anchor light paints his skin in soft gold, highlighting the edges of his strong shoulders, wet curls plastered against his temples, the long line of his neck where droplets trail down and disappear beneath his collar. I try not to stare, but it's impossible not to notice everything now. Every breath. Every shift. Every space where his body brushes just close enough to remind me I'm aware of him in a way that feels a little reckless and far too late to stop.

I crouch beside him, pretending to busy myself with a fin strap I already loosened, and feel the words gathering before I can fully catch them.

"I've never felt anything like that before," I say quietly, unsure at first whether I'm speaking aloud or just thinking too loudly inside my own head. "The dive, I mean. And... everything else."

I keep my gaze low, not ready yet to see the expression on his face. He doesn't respond, but I can feel his attention shift toward me. Not with his body—he's still working through the routine motions of breaking down equipment but with something else, something quieter and more consuming. That Jorge kind of focus, the kind that feels like being watched and seen in the same breath.

"I know this probably isn't what you want to hear," I continue, a nervous breath catching behind the words. "And I know I'm just... visiting. Passing through. You probably get this kind of thing all the time."

I glance at him, then away, my fingers now twisting the same strap too tightly.

"But this—whatever this is doesn't feel like nothing to me. I don't think it's just the water or the setting or some cliché vacation moment. I've felt those before, and this... isn't that."

I feel the heat rising across my cheeks, the way it always does when I speak too quickly or too honestly, and for a second, I consider backpedaling, laughing it off, stuffing it back inside before I lose too much of myself in the telling. But I can't. Because it's already there between us, too real to unsay.

"I don't even know what I'm asking for," I admit, my voice softening again, "or if I'm asking for anything at all. I just know I feel something. Something real. And I wanted you to know that."

Finally, I lift my eyes.

Jorge is still. His hands have stilled, his breath a little slower than it was a moment ago, and his eyes are dark, steady, unreadable they are locked onto mine. There's no immediate reaction, no kind reassurance or easy letdown. No movement at all.

Only silence.

But it isn't the kind that hurts. Not yet.

It's the kind that holds. That stretches and curls into something heavier, more complicated than a yes or a no. A silence full of weight and want and things neither of us has figured out how to name.

And it's the way he's looking at me like he's trying not to feel everything I just confessed, and failing that sends a shiver through me, low and slow and aching.

My chest tightens. My breath stumbles. My heart pushes up against my ribs like it's trying to reach for something just out of reach.

He still hasn't said a word.

But I can feel it; the shift in the air, the electricity humming beneath the surface of his silence and I know I've just crossed a line that can't be uncrossed.

Chapter 8

Jorge

H er confession hits me like a tidal wave.

I've been resisting her, telling myself that I'm here to do a job, that I shouldn't get too close, that this *thing* between us is nothing but a momentary distraction.

But now... now I'm realizing how much of a lie that is.

We've just come up from the night dive, the dark water still clinging to my skin, the boat rocking gently beneath us as we head back to the dock. The hum of the engine fills the silence between us, but it's not enough to drown out the way my pulse is thumping in my ears.

I glance over at Piper. She's standing by the rail, wrapped tightly in a towel, her wetsuit still on underneath, hugging her body in all the right places. The way it clings to her curves every inch of her waist, her hips, the gentle dip of her collarbones making it impossible for me to look away. The damp towel around her shoulders only makes her more exposed, her body heat radiating off her in the cool night air.

She's beautiful. And she knows it.

But it's not just the way she looks, it's the way she carries herself, the quiet confidence that comes through in every small movement. Even with the tension in her face, even with the quiet uncertainty that I can see in the way she's chewing her lip, she's still... her. Unapologetically real, and it's getting harder for me to push it away.

I feel it, too. The pull. The desire to be close, to hear more from her. To know *everything* about this woman who's completely unsettled me.

Then, just like that, she turns toward me, her voice soft but steady. "Jorge, I... I don't know if I can keep pretending."

It catches me off guard, and I'm suddenly unable to breathe. Her words hang in the air between us, cutting through the engine's drone and everything I've been trying to ignore. She's not looking at me now, not waiting for a response, her fingers tracing the edge of the boat as if she's too afraid to meet my gaze.

Her confession sinks in, deeper than I want it to.

I've been telling myself I could keep my distance, that this whatever this is or was is just temporary. That I could avoid this whole damn thing and stay focused on the job. But now?

Now, it's impossible.

Her words shake me, crack through the wall I've carefully built around myself, and suddenly I'm *here*, standing on the edge with her, not knowing what comes next. I want to pull back. I want to say something, anything that will make this all go away. But I don't.

I can't.

I know I should keep my distance. I know I'm not supposed to get involved, not like this. She's a guest. A tourist. And I'm the guy who works here, keeping to the shadows, out of sight, avoiding attachments.

But Piper's different. She makes it impossible to just let this go.

The problem is, I'm not sure I want to.

The boat slows to a stop, the gentle hum of the engine fading as we reach the dock. The water's calm tonight, the reflection of the moonlight shimmering off the surface. It's peaceful here, but I can feel the tension in the air—thick, almost suffocating.

She's quiet now, looking out at the water as if she's not sure what to say. I know exactly how she feels.

We both know we've crossed some kind of line tonight. The weight of it sits heavy between us, unspoken. And now, neither of us knows what to do with it.

I reach out and steady the boat as it bumps against the dock, grabbing the rope to tie it down. When I finish, I turn to her, offering her a hand. She takes it, and the simple touch feels like more than just a greeting it's a connection, something deeper, undeniable.

We step off the boat together, the cool night air greeting us as we walk toward the dock. I keep my distance, but not by much, our shoulders brushing every few steps. I can't stop noticing the way she moves so easy, unhurried, like she knows exactly where she's going.

We reach the dive shop in silence. The dim light inside spills out onto the dock, warm and inviting, but it feels almost too intimate now. We don't need words; we don't need explanations. The hours of conversation we've shared earlier in the dive shop are still hanging between us, and I can feel it in the way she's looking at me.

We step inside, and the door creaks behind us as I flick on the light. The dive shop is quiet now, the soft hum of the fan and the smell of saltwater lingering in the air. Piper glances around, her eyes taking in the space like she's never really seen it before.

I motion toward the old couch in the corner. "Make yourself comfortable. Want something to drink?"

Her gaze meets mine, and for a brief second, there's a shift—a wordless agreement, a silent understanding that tonight is different. She nods, just slightly, and I grab a couple of beers from the fridge. We sit across from each other, the tension between us palpable now, but still unspoken.

We talk. And talk.

About everything and nothing. About the island, about diving, about the things we left behind. The tension builds with every word, a slow burn that I can feel in the pit of my stomach. The conversation flows easily at first, but it doesn't stay easy for long.

She laughs, and it's light, full of life, something I didn't expect to hear after everything. The sound cuts through the space between us, making my chest tighten. She's real, and I'm starting to feel that more than I ever wanted to admit.

I catch myself staring at her, drawn in by her vibrant energy, her genuine curiosity. There's something about her that makes it impossible to look away.

And as the hours pass, the weight of everything between us only deepens. Neither of us says what we're both thinking. Neither of us acknowledges the pull that's been building since the moment we met.

But it's there.

And I know it's only a matter of time before one of us says it out loud.

As we talk, I begin to realize something I didn't expect. Piper isn't just some tourist passing through. She's not here for a brief escape, not just for the thrill of a few dives and a couple of snapshots to show off later. No, there's so much more to her than that.

She's smart. And funny. And more adventurous than I thought. Her sense of humor is sharp, but it's the kind that sneaks up on you it's effortless, spontaneous, like she's comfortable enough in her own skin to let go and *be* herself. And when she laughs, it's genuine—unforced and full of life, a sound that's impossible not to get lost in.

But what really catches me is how much depth there is behind those eyes. When she talks about her art, I see the passion in her, the need to create, to express what the world makes her feel. It's more than just a hobby to her; it's part of who she is, like she's chasing something deeper than any dive could bring her. I've known artists before, but the way Piper speaks about her work, it's clear she's connected to something that runs through her veins. It's raw, real, and incredibly *alive*.

Then, as the night stretches on, she starts talking about her travels and all the places she's been, the risks she's taken, and the adventures that have shaped her. She's not just someone who's here for the vacation, for the easy fun of the island. She's lived, really lived, in a way most people just dream about. She's thrown herself into situations that would make most people balk. And she's done it with an openness, a fearlessness that makes me want to know everything about her.

She's not here just to escape. She's searching for something, or maybe for herself. And I can't help but be drawn to that. She's not just some tourist passing through. She's someone with a quiet strength, a drive to experience the world and understand it in ways I never expected.

And in this moment, as I listen to her talk and watch the way her eyes light up when she's passionate about something, I realize it again. She's not just here to take from this place. She's here because she has something more to offer than most people ever will.

Piper isn't just a tourist.

She's a force. And I'm starting to wonder if I'm falling for it—or her.

I can feel it at that moment. The one I've been trying to ignore, trying to resist, to convince myself I shouldn't cross that line. But here we are, sitting on this worn-out couch in the dim light of the dive shop, our words fading into a quiet hum, the weight of everything we've said and everything we haven't hanging between us.

I've never felt like this before. The pull. The raw electricity that's been crackling in the air, building between us since the second I laid eyes on her.

Her eyes are locked on mine now, dark and intense, and for a second, everything else fades away. The noise of the island, the boats, the tourists, the dive shop—it all disappears. There's just her. Just the way her lips part slightly, the way she's breathing a little faster, the way her gaze flicks to my mouth before meeting my eyes again.

She wants this, too.

The realization hits me harder than any dive.

Without thinking, I move closer. It's like the world has paused, holding its breath. The space between us closes in an instant, and before I can stop myself, my hand is cupping the side of her face, pulling her toward me. Her breath hitches, her eyes flutter closed, and for the briefest moment, I hesitate.

But I can't resist anymore.

I kiss her.

And it's everything I didn't know I wanted. It's raw, hungry, and impossibly soft all at once. Her lips are warm, inviting, and I feel her body lean into mine, soft curves fitting against me like we've been doing this for years. Her breath mingles with mine, the scent of saltwater and something sweeter on her skin, and it takes everything in me not to pull her closer, deepen the kiss, lose myself in it.

I'm not thinking about anything else. Not the dive, not the job, not the rules I've been telling myself to follow. There's only her. Only this.

She responds to me like she's been waiting for this, too, her fingers finding my chest, pressing against the fabric of my shirt, and I feel the heat between us intensify. Her mouth moves against mine, slow at first, exploring, as if she's making sure I'm real, as if she's making sure this is real.

It's everything I didn't know I wanted. It's her warmth, her taste, the rush of adrenaline that comes with crossing that line, knowing we can't go back. And I don't want to.

The kiss deepens, and with it, the world around us starts to melt away. There's nothing else now, no distractions, no regrets. Just the taste of her, soft and addictive, the feel of her against me, the warmth spreading between us like a fire catching in dry wood.

I move my hand to her back, pulling her closer, and she doesn't resist. Her body is warm and pliant, pressing against mine, and for a moment, I lose track of everything else. The dive shop, the moonlight outside, the sound of the world continuing on—none of it matters.

Her hands roam carefully over my chest, exploring, as if she's testing the waters, unsure but wanting more. The soft brush of her fingertips against my skin sends a wave of heat through me, and I find myself leaning in again, kissing her harder this time, a little less gentle, a little more desperate.

Her lips part beneath mine, and I feel her breath catch, a soft sigh escaping her, stirring something deeper in me. There's a softness in her I hadn't noticed before, a vulnerability that makes me ache with a longing I didn't expect.

I pull away just enough to look at her, her eyes wide, her cheeks flushed, her chest rising and falling with every breath. She looks at me, and I see the same fire in her eyes, the same mix of want and uncertainty.

"You sure?" I ask, my voice rough, trying to steady myself. "Because once we go there..."

She doesn't answer with words. She just pulls me back to her, her lips finding mine again, more insistent now. No hesitation. No fear.

I let myself fall into it. Let myself fall into her.

Her hands slide down the side of my tank top, tentative at first, then more certain as she inches closer. And I feel myself reacting every nerve alive, every inch of me awakes with the heat between us. My hands shake slightly as I run them down her sides, feeling the smoothness of her skin where the wetsuit has been pulled halfway down, exposing her bare upper body.

It's slow, exploratory. We're testing the waters, neither of us fully committing, yet neither of us pulling away. It's all new, all thrilling, as though this is a dance we've both been waiting for, but neither of us knows the steps.

I lean back just enough to look at her again. Her lips are swollen, her eyes heavy with desire, but there's something else there too, something vulnerable, like she's giving me a piece of herself she's never given anyone before.

And I can't help but feel it, the weight of it. The power of what's happening between us.

"Piper," I whisper, my breath shaky. "Are you sure?"

She meets my gaze, her expression soft but sure. "Yes," she breathes, voice barely a whisper, but it hits me harder than anything.

I lean in again, kissing her slowly, deeply, tasting the softness of her lips. She melts into me, her body pressing closer, the warmth of her skin flooding my senses. My hands move down her back, tracing the lines of her body with careful intention, feeling the subtle curve of her spine, the soft dip of her waist.

She responds to me in kind, her hands slipping under my tank top, the coolness of her touch against my skin sending a shiver through me. The feeling of her fingertips against my body makes my chest tighten, my pulse quickens, but I force myself to stay present, to take this one slow, careful step at a time.

Her lips move to my neck, soft and slow, the warmth of her breath against my skin sending a spark of heat through me. I gasp softly, the feeling of her mouth on me so tender, so new. She takes her time, her hands gliding over my chest, feeling the muscles beneath my skin, exploring, discovering. Each touch is gentle, deliberate, like she's memorizing every part of me.

I gently pull the wetsuit down, exposing more of her skin, and the feeling of her bare body against mine makes my heart race. I pause for a moment, just taking her in; her eyes, half-lidded with desire, the flush of color in her cheeks, the way her body moves under my touch. She's beautiful. But there's something deeper, something more, in the way she's letting me in, trusting me in this space between us.

I move slowly, my hands exploring the newly exposed skin of her waist and stomach, feeling the softness of her body, the subtle curve of her hips. I trace the lines of her ribs with my fingertips, feeling her breathe in, a slight shiver running through her as I touch her.

Her hands slide down to my shorts, unfastening them carefully, slowly, the same deliberate pace. We're not rushing this. Every touch, every movement is filled with anticipation, the quiet understanding between us that this is our moment.Our first step into something more.

I help her slip my shorts off, and for a moment, we just pause. I look at her, and she looks back at me, her eyes searching, searching for something in mine. It's like we're both looking for permission, for confirmation that this is real, that this is what we both want.

I kiss her again, slow and soft, pulling her closer until her body is flush against mine, our skin meeting, warm and eager. I can feel her heart pounding against mine, and I know she's feeling the same fire, the same need.

I guide her gently back onto the couch, the soft cushions beneath us, and I lean over her, kissing her neck, her shoulders, tasting her skin like it's something I can't get enough of. She's soft beneath me, her body responding to mine with the same urgency, the same hunger.

Slowly, carefully, I move against her, my hands exploring, my lips following the lines of her body, discovering every inch, every curve. Her hands find my back, pulling me closer, urging me on, but we don't rush. We don't need to.

This is our first time, and it's everything. It's tender, it's real, it's filled with all the emotions we've been hiding, all the desire we've kept buried.

I take my time, moving with her, feeling every inch of her skin against mine, the way she responds to me, the way her body fits against me so perfectly. Every movement between us feels deliberate, a dance of sorts. Our bodies are pressed together now, skin on skin, and I can feel the warmth of her body, the softness of her skin beneath my hands.

I lean down, kissing her again, the taste of her lingering on my lips. Her hands are everywhere from my back, to my chest, running through my hair and each touch sends a shiver of desire through me, but I hold myself back, taking my time, savoring the way her body moves against mine.

I feel her legs shift, wrapping around my waist, pulling me closer, and the sensation is electric. The heat between us intensifies, but I force myself to slow down, to feel every inch of her body, every part of this moment. Her skin is soft, warm, and she's gasping beneath me, her hands trailing down my sides, exploring the muscles of my back.

I'm painfully aware of the way my body reacts to hers and how my heart races, how my pulse quickens, how every inch of me craves more. But I hold back, leaning into the kiss, my hand sliding down her side, feeling the curve of her waist, the softness of her hips.

She moves beneath me, her body arching into mine, and I can feel her heat, the desire in the way she pulls me closer, the way her body fits perfectly against mine. I shift, and she follows, her legs wrapping tighter around my waist, urging me on, but I take it slow. There's no rush, no need to push it's just quiet, the slow buildup of everything we've been holding back.

Her breath comes in soft gasps, her chest rising and falling beneath me, and I can feel her heartbeat against mine, racing in time with the rhythm of our bodies. I kiss down her neck, my lips trailing over her soft skin, tasting the salt of the ocean that clings to her, mingling with the warmth of her body...

I hear her sigh, fingers digging into my back as I move lower, lips tracing the dip between her ribs. Her skin tastes like salt and something sweeter—something *hers*—and when she shifts beneath me, hips lifting just slightly, I lose the last sliver of control I'd been clinging to.

She wants this. Wants *me*. Not in some passing way.

In the way that wrecks you.

I drag my mouth slowly along her stomach, every inch of her like a goddamn revelation. Her breath hitches when I graze my teeth along the edge of her hip, and I feel her thighs tighten around me, her legs wrapping higher. She's not shy at allshe's starving, same as me.

"Jorge," she breathes, and my name in her voice does something to me—pulls something raw to the surface.

I look up. She's propped on her elbows, lips parted, eyes glassy and dark, watching me like I'm already inside her.

"You sure?" I ask again, voice low, ragged, but steady.

She doesn't answer with words.

She sits up, grabs me by the back of the neck, and pulls me into a kiss that *ends* the question.

It's messy. Hot. Her tongue finds mine with a boldness that catches me off guard and makes my cock throb against the seam of my shorts. She grinds up against me, and I lose it.I grab her hips, roll her onto her back again, and settle between her thighs, the pressure perfect, maddening, not nearly enough.

She pulls her tank top off like she's done thinking, done waiting, and holy *fuck*—

My breath punches out of me.

Her body is everything I imagined—and I've imagined it more than I'll ever admit. Tight curves, soft skin, and nipples already hard as I lean down and take one into my mouth.

She gasps, arches, fingers flying to my hair, tugging like she's trying to anchor herself.

I suck gently at first, then harder, feeling the way her hips twitch under me.

"God," she whispers, and I hum against her chest, switching sides, sliding my hand down her belly at the same time, fingertips slipping under the waistband of her shorts.

She moans when I touch her. Just a single stroke, over her underwear, but it's soaked.

"Jesus, Piper," I breathe, voice rough. "You're already this wet for me?"

"Since the boat," she says, shameless, breathless. "I couldn't stop thinking about you."

That breaks something loose in me.

I tug her shorts off, slow but deliberate, dragging them past her thighs, her knees, her ankles. She kicks them aside, bold and bare and fucking *perfect* in the moonlight.

And when I dip my head between her thighs and finally taste her?

She cries out, hand flying to her mouth.

But I want to *hear* her.

I push her hand away gently, lock eyes with her, and slide my tongue deep—slow, slow, then up, circling her clit, teasing, learning how she likes it. Her hips roll, chasing it, chasing me.

"Don't stop," she begs, voice cracked open.

I don't.

I suck, I flick, I stroke her with my tongue like I already know every part of her and by the way she grabs the back of my head, trembling, legs tightening around me like a vise.

She's close.

"Jorge—fuck—I'm—"

I slide two fingers into her, curling just right, and she comes hard biting her lip, arching beneath me, her body clenching around me like it doesn't want to let go.

I keep going. Slow it down, then build again. I want her ruined for anyone else.

By the time she comes the second time, she's shaking.

I crawl up her body, kiss her breathless, let her taste herself on my tongue. Her hands find my waistband, tugging it down, wrapping around me and I nearly lose it right then.

"You sure?" I whisper again, forehead against hers.

She kisses me like a promise.

"I want you," she says. "Now."

And with that, I press into her slow, deep and we both gasp at the stretch, the heat, the *rightness* of it.

And for the first time in years, I stop thinking.

I just *feel*.

I press into her slowly, and it's like the world narrows to the heat between us.

She's tight ,hot and slick pulsing around me as her thighs lift, wrapping around my waist. I bite down hard on a groan, my arms trembling from how good she feels. It's everything I expected and nothing like I imagined.

She clutches at my shoulders, nails biting into my skin in the best kind of way. Her head falls back as I sink in deeper, inch by inch, giving her time to adjust but she doesn't pull back.

She pulls me closer.

Deeper.

"Don't hold back," she whispers, voice low and wrecked.

And I don't.

I thrust into her fully, burying myself inside with one smooth, firm stroke, and her cry rips through the quiet night like a fuse catching flame. I pause there, chest pressed to hers my forehead against her temple. I'm trying to hold on to this moment, this first, perfect *collapse* of boundaries.

"Jesus, Piper," I breathe against her skin. "You feel... unreal."

Her hips rise to meet mine and I start to move slow and deep at first, dragging out every inch, every roll of our bodies like it's the first dance we've ever known. She matches me perfectly, her rhythm syncing with mine, her fingers gripping my back like she never wants to let go.

Her mouth finds mine, and we kiss through it, it's messy, open-mouthed, greedy. She tastes like sweat, salt, and surrender. I slide a hand beneath her ass, lifting her higher, angling her just right, and the sound she makes when I hit deeper makes my whole body tighten.

She moans again, louder, unfiltered. "*Fuck, Jorge...*"

I slam into her harder, rolling my hips, driving deeper, again and again until our bodies are slick with sweat, the sounds of skin and breath echoing across the dock. I can't stop kissing her—her mouth, her jaw, her neck, the hollow of her throat. She moans my name over and over like it's the only word she knows.

She's trembling beneath me, close again.

I reach between us and rub her clit, slow, tight circles, and she comes *hard*, nails digging into my shoulders, thighs squeezing around me as she shakes under the weight of it.

She says my name like a broken prayer, and I lose whatever control I had left.

I thrust into her harder, chasing that edge with everything I've got, and she holds me through it her hands in my hair, her lips on my jaw, whispering *yes* and *more* and *don't stop* until I finally break.

I groan her name into her shoulder, thrust once, twice more and then come deep inside her, shuddering, gasping, every muscle locked as the release crashes through me like a wave I didn't see coming.

We collapse into each other, breathless.

Sweaty.

Spent.

I stay inside her, head buried in her neck, both of us trembling in the aftershock. Her fingers draw slow lines down my spine, soft and grounding, and I don't think I've ever felt this close to another human in my life.

We don't speak.

We don't have to.

Her heartbeat flutters beneath my lips as I kiss the spot just below her ear, slow and reverent.

And I know, as I hold her in the dark—

This was never going to be just one night.

Not with her.

Not after this.

The air around us is still, thick with the scent of sex and salt and warm night.

Piper's chest rises and falls beneath me, her skin sticky against mine, her fingers now moving in soft, lazy patterns over my back. No words. Just breath. Just the echo of what we just did, still vibrating in the silence between us like a quiet, shared secret.

I lift my head to look at her.

She's staring up at the stars, hair tangled across the blanket, lips parted slightly, a tiny, contented smile ghosting there like she doesn't know it's happening.

Beautiful.

Uncomplicated, for once.

She glances at me and her smile widens, soft and slow, and something inside me shifts again—something I don't have the language for. Something dangerous, maybe.

I press a kiss to her shoulder, then settle back down, one arm draped around her waist, fingers drawing circles low on her stomach. She hums, barely audible, and I feel her body melt deeper into mine.

This... feels like peace.

Not just the silence. Not just the sex. But the *after*. The weightless, anchored calm that only comes when your body stops fighting, when everything goes quiet in a way it hasn't in years.

I should get up. Pull the blanket over her, clean us up, say something casual that resets the line we just obliterated.

But I don't move.

I stay pressed against her, my hand splayed across her belly, feeling the warmth of her skin radiate into mine like we're still connected from the inside out.

And I wonder for the first time in a long time if I even *want* to pull back.

She shifts slightly, nestles into me, and mumbles something soft, barely a breath. I don't catch all of it. Just my name and maybe *don't go.*

And I won't. Not tonight.

I kiss her temple, close my eyes, and let the night swallow me whole.

But just as the edge of sleep starts to pull me under, something sharp flutters at the back of my mind.

A memory, maybe.

Or a warning.

That nothing on this island, nothing this good   comes without a cost.

And whatever this is between us?

It's already deeper than I meant it to be.

Chapter 9

Piper

I wake up warm.

Not just the kind of warmth that came from the sun filtering through the gauzy curtains or the distant hum of island heat already thickening the air but the kind that came from being wrapped in someone else. Jorge's arm was draped heavy over my waist, his chest pressed against my back, his breath slow and even in that just-before-waking rhythm. One of his legs was tangled with mine, anchoring me to the bed, to him, to this little cocoon of impossible intimacy.

I blinked up at the ceiling, still hazy, still floating in that in-between space where dreams and memories blurred together. My skin tingled, still sensitive in places. My inner thighs ached in the best kind of way. His voice echoed softly in my mind low, rough, full of want. My name had never sounded like that before.

God, the way he touched me. The way he looked at me, like I wasn't just someone he wanted I was someone he *saw*.

For a moment, I just lay there, eyes closed, soaking it all in. The weight of his arm, the comfort of his warmth, the scent of salt and skin and something I was starting to think of as just... Jorge. I didn't want to move. I didn't want the moment to end.

But underneath all that softness, there was a flicker of something else. A tight little knot behind my ribs.

Was this real?

Not the night, we *definitely* didn't imagine that but the *rest* of it. The part where he stayed. The part where I woke up still in his bed, still in his arms.

Was this just a vacation thing? A beautiful, sun-drenched fling we'd both remember fondly when we went back to our actual lives? Or had something shifted?

Was I reading too much into it?

I didn't *feel* casual. I felt cracked open.

I shifted slightly, careful not to wake him. He didn't stir. My heart, that traitorous thing, fluttered anyway. He looked peaceful, maybe even a little vulnerable. The sharp lines of his face had softened, his brow smooth, mouth slack. Without the gruff exterior and all that bossy dive instructor energy, he looked younger. More like the boy he must've been before life started piling weight on his shoulders.

And it hit me, hard and sudden, that I didn't *want* this to be just a vacation thing.

Which was terrifying.

Because I didn't know what Jorge wanted. He wasn't exactly big on declarations. And it wasn't like I was in a place to make promises either. I had a return flight, a job, a whole messy life back home. Whatever this was, it lived in borrowed time.

Still, I couldn't stop myself from wondering: Did last night feel like this for him too?

Did he fall asleep thinking about what came next... or just about how good it had been?

Was I the exception or just a moment?

Behind me, Jorge stirred.

His arm shifted, strong and sure, sliding around my waist with the kind of instinct that said he wasn't quite awake yet but already didn't want me to move. A deep, contented sound rumbled from his chest, vibrating against my spine. Then came the slow, warm exhale against my neck. And finally, finally a kiss. Lazy, unhurried, pressed right where my shoulder met my throat.

"Morning," he rasped, voice thick with sleep and heat and something that sounded suspiciously like contentment.

I couldn't help the smile that stretched across my lips. "Hey."

He shifted again, this time rolling to his back and pulling me with him like I was something precious. I ended up draped half over his chest, thigh hooked over his, cheek resting against warm, bare skin. His heart beat steady beneath my ear. His fingers started a lazy circuit over my back, tracing invisible patterns that made my whole-body hum.

"How long have you been awake?" he murmured.

"Not long."

"You were thinking," he said, not a question. "I could feel it."

I lifted my head, met his eyes. They were soft in the morning light, a stormy kind of hazel, still heavy-lidded with sleep but alert now and focused entirely on me.

"Yeah," I admitted. "It's kind of my thing."

He brushed a strand of hair off my cheek. "Wanna tell me what about?"

I hesitated. I wasn't ready to spill everything. Not yet. But I didn't want to lie, either.

"I was wondering if this... if *we*... is just part of the trip. A vacation thing."

He didn't flinch. Didn't look away. His hand kept moving in slow, grounding strokes.

"Does it feel like that to you?" he asked, voice low, careful.

I swallowed. "No. That's the problem."

A beat passed. Then he smiled. It was small, but real.

"Good," he said.

And it was such a Jorge answer that I laughed, the knot in my chest loosening just a little.

We fell into a soft silence. I let my eyes close again, body molded to his. I hadn't meant to fall into him like this, hadn't planned for any of it. But it felt... inevitable now. Like a tide that had been rising the whole time.

Eventually, he spoke again, voice still hushed. "You know, I don't usually sleep in."

I raised a brow. "No?"

"No. I'm up with the sun. Half the time I'm yelling at Lester by seven."

I smiled against his chest. "So why are you still here?"

His hand slid into my hair, fingers threading through gently. "Because you're here."

I didn't breathe for a second. Just let the words settle in my chest like warm stones. Simple. Honest. Undeniable.

"So, what would you be doing today if I wasn't here?" I asked, needing the ground again, even as part of me floated.

He gave a lazy little grunt. "Checking tanks. Fixing that damn engine on the skiff. Probably arguing with Mark about something dumb."

"Sounds thrilling."

"It's glamorous, what can I say?" He chuckled, then sobered slightly. "I used to think I'd leave. See the world. Work boats out in Fiji or Mozambique. I had this idea that I'd chase the bluest water I could find."

I propped myself up on an elbow, curious. "So, what happened?"

He shrugged. "My dad got sick. I took over the shop. And then it was just... easier to stay. People needed me here. And eventually, I stopped asking myself what I wanted."

That last part landed with a thud in my chest.

I reached up, ran my fingers along his jaw. "Do you still think about leaving?"

He looked at me for a long moment. "Lately... I think about *why* I'd leave. And whether I'd want to take someone with me."

The air between us turned electric but tender, yes, but charged with something more. Possibility.

"What about you?" he asked, eyes never leaving mine. "What's your blue water?"

I exhaled slowly, heart full and aching. "A messy little studio. Canvas everywhere. Paint on my clothes. Making things that make people feel something."

He smiled, like he could see it. Like he could *see me.*

"You could do that," he said softly. "You *should.*"

I bit my lip. "It's not that easy."

"No," he agreed. "But maybe it's time you stop telling yourself it's impossible."

God. The way he looked at me, it wasn't infatuation, It wasn't just post-sex glow. It was a belief. Steady. Unshaken. Like he saw all the broken, half-formed pieces of me and didn't flinch.

He pulled me in again, kissed my forehead like it was instinct. And I let him, curling into the quiet safety of his chest.

Maybe this wasn't just a fling.

Maybe it was the beginning of something neither of us had planned but both of us desperately needed.

Lying there, skin to skin with him, I felt it.

That slow, terrifying pull in my chest.

Like something inside me was shifting—quietly, irrevocably. Like the ground I thought I'd been standing on had tilted without warning, and I didn't know whether to hold my breath or jump.

I was falling for him.

Not a crush. Not a fling. Not just the breathless aftermath of good sex and soft sheets and sleepy smiles.

Something real.

I felt it in the way I watched him sleep—like I was memorizing his face, the little furrow between his brows, the flutter of his lashes, the shape of his mouth when he wasn't using it to argue or tease or kiss me breathless. I felt it in the weight of his hand splayed across my back, the way his fingers moved like he didn't even know he was touching me, like it had become instinct.

And I felt it in the ache blooming low in my chest. The one that whispered, this won't last.

That's when it hit me, with all the subtlety of a slap to the face:

My vacation is ending soon.

There was a literal timer on this thing between us. Days. Hours, if I really thought about it. And when the countdown reached zero, I'd have to pack my bags, zip up my suitcase, and leave this behind like it was just a chapter in someone else's story.

And maybe that was always the plan. Maybe that was what it *should* be. A perfect little escape. Something I'd remember when the real world got too loud. A beautiful mistake, if I wanted to call it that.

But that wasn't what this felt like.

It felt like something I'd be sorry to walk away from. Like something I wasn't done with yet.

And the worst part? I didn't even know what it was to him.

Was it just a vacation thing?

Had I become convenient because I was here, because we kept running into each other, because I wore sundresses and laughed too loud and looked at him like I wanted more even if I hadn't said it out loud?

The thing no one tells you about close proximity is how fast it happens.

You go from strangers to something else in a blink of an eye because you're thrown together in all the ways that matter. You share routines and silences and sunburns. You eat breakfast at the same bar and end up floating in the ocean side by side. You get used to their voice, their rhythms, their stubborn little habits. You learn what makes them roll their eyes and what makes them smile when they think no one's looking.

You fall quietly, fully and stupidly because you've stopped pretending not to care.

I hadn't planned this. I wasn't supposed to *want* anything. I came here to breathe again, to remember who I was when I wasn't stuck in emails and rent and expectations. I came here to be someone else for a little while. Someone lighter. Someone temporary.

But Jorge made me feel more *me* than I had in years.

And now? Now I didn't know what to do with that.

Because if I asked for more, I could ruin it.

And if I said nothing, I'd lose something I wasn't ready to let go of.

So I stayed quiet, curled against his chest, listening to his heartbeat like it could drown out the noise in my head. His fingers were still in my hair. His breathing was calm. He had no idea the storm happening just inches away.

And I hated that part of me; the scared part, the one that would rather stay silent than risk falling harder.

But maybe that's what love was too. Not just the warm, perfect moments in tangled sheets but the fear, the longing. The *choice* to say something anyway.

And I wasn't there yet.

Not quite.

But I was close.

So close it hurt.

We were still wrapped in morning warmth on his porch, sunlight just starting to creep across the floorboards, when I turned toward him with my best innocent smile.

"You should skip work today."

Jorge didn't even look up from the coffee mug in his hands. "No, I shouldn't."

I shifted closer on the bench, letting my bare thigh brush against his. "Come on. One day. Just us."

He tilted his head, finally glancing at me. "I've got a full boat this morning."

"I know." I nudged him with my shoulder. "But hear me out, you've done what, a thousand dives? You've seen every reef, every sponge, every dramatic fish in a bad mood."

He gave a reluctant smile. "And I still have six guests who want their money's worth."

"Lester can take them."

He actually laughed at that. "Lester once forgot to bring *air*. Actual tanks. We had to double back mid-channel."

"Okay, so maybe not Lester solo, but someone else? Isn't there, like, a substitute dive instructor hotline?"

He took a sip of his coffee, clearly amused. "Is this your subtle way of telling me you want another date?"

"This is my not-so-subtle way of telling you I want to spend the entire day with you without a wetsuit or a dive briefing or people asking you how many barracudas are in the bay."

He turned, finally facing me fully. His gaze dropped to my mouth. "And what would this imaginary day look like?"

"I don't know," I said, playing it casual even though my heart was hammering. "We could walk into town, steal mango slices from that little fruit stand. Get empanadas. Make fun of over-priced beach art."

"Tempting."

"We could even take a nap later," I added, lowering my voice. "Or not nap."

His gaze darkened, just slightly.

I smiled.

"Skip with me," I whispered. "You never do anything for yourself. Just once. Be irresponsible."

He leaned back, watching me like he was trying not to be swayed. "What if someone notices?"

"Let them," I said, voice soft. "Let them wonder where you went."

He didn't answer right away. His hand moved, brushing my knee—slow, deliberate, warm.

Then he sighed, rubbing a hand over the back of his neck. "I can't cancel the morning dives. I gave my word."

My face fell before I could stop it.

"But," he added, eyes locked on mine, "I'll cancel the afternoon."

I blinked. "Really?"

He nodded. "I'll move some things around. Lester can handle the return gear and the night dive prep. I'll be back around noon."

A flush of something warm and tight bloomed in my chest. "You promise?"

"I do," he said, a little hoarse.

Then he reached for me, pulled me into his lap like it was nothing. Like we did this every day.

"You're dangerous," he muttered against my shoulder.

"And yet here you are," I whispered, wrapping my arms around him.

He just held me for a moment, long and solid, like he already knew that one afternoon wasn't going to be enough.

Back in my room, the silence was jarring.

It settled over me like a second skin. Still and sterile, too bright, too quiet after the cocoon of Jorge's sheets and steady breathing. The bed hadn't been touched since yesterday. The air conditioning hummed faintly, indifferent. Nothing here smelled like him. Nothing felt like him. The space, once mine, now felt foreign, like I was standing on the other side of something and couldn't figure out how to go back.

I peeled off his shirt it's soft, sun-faded cotton with a faint scent of salt and skin and I let it fall to the floor. My reflection in the mirror caught me by surprise. My lips were still swollen. My hair was a wild mess. Faint bruises dotted the curve of my shoulder, the inside of my thigh. Ghosts of his mouth. His hands.

The steam hits me first, the air thick, warm, curling up my thighs and wrapping around my ribs like a lover's breath. I close the door behind me and step fully under the spray, letting the water crash against my collarbone, run in rivulets between my breasts, and trace the soft curve of my stomach. My eyes close. My head falls back.

I swear I can still feel him.

Jorge.

His hands. His mouth. His body, heavy and hot and moving through me like he knew exactly where I broke and exactly how to break me again.

I press my palms flat to the tile, grounding myself, but the water doesn't calm me. It stokes the heat still simmering under my skin, low and urgent and *deep*. My nipples tighten in the cool air between droplets, begging to be touched. My thighs clench with a desperate ache that's been building since the moment I woke up alone and aching.

I bring my hand up slowly, running it over my breast, cupping it fully then squeezing, thumb brushing over my nipple until I hiss through my teeth. My hips shift, just a little, instinctive.

I need more.

My other hand trails down, between my thighs. I part them slightly, guiding my fingers over my slick folds starting light at first, like a tease. My middle finger glides between them, dipping just barely inside, enough to make my mouth fall open on a breathless moan.

I'm so wet. Not just from the water.

From the memory of his voice in my ear.

From the way he held my legs open and said "Stay like that. Let me taste you."

I circle my clit, slow at first—little, deliberate swirls that make my knees threaten to buckle. My face twists, eyebrows pinching together, lips parting in a gasp I can't contain. My whole body is leaning into it now, rolling gently against my hand as I press harder, drawing tighter circles, breath growing ragged and short.

I whisper his name.

"Jorge..."

It leaves my lips like a plea.

My free hand slides back to my breast, tugging harder now, matching the rhythm between my legs. I roll my nipple between two fingers, imagining his teeth there only a graze, then a bite. My mouth drops open wider, head tilted back against the tile, water cascading over my chest, my belly, my thighs, while my fingers slip lower again.

This time I don't stop.

I slide two fingers inside me—slow, deep, and I *moan*.

Loud.

The stretch makes me shudder, hips jerking forward, clenching around my own hand like I'm trying to drag him into me again. My face flushes with heat, my eyes half-lidded, mouth parted, lips slick with steam and want. My expression is a wrecked, open thing—pure need. I can feel my jaw trembling, the way my breath staggers with every thrust of my fingers.

I fuck myself slow, deep, curling inside just the way he did. My thumb brushes my clit and my body jolts, hips bucking, breath catching.

The pressure is building fast so fast a low burn curling deep in my core, spreading outward like a wave gathering strength.

I press harder. Grind my palm against myself. My body moves in tight, desperate rolls, fucking my own hand now like I can't stop, like I'll die if I don't come.

"Fuck," I cry out, barely more than a gasp. "Fuck, Jorge, *please—*"

My voice is high, breaking, shaking.

I'm chasing it now. Losing control.

I feel my eyes flutter shut, head thrown back, mouth open as the orgasm coils so tight I can barely breathe.

And then it hits.

Like a goddamn storm.

My whole-body locks.

My back arches.

My fingers stay buried deep as the first wave crashes through me; it's hot, wet, violent. I *scream* into the steam, thighs clenching, muscles seizing around my hand. Pleasure rips through me in waves, shudder after shudder, raw and relentless. My breath breaks apart in sobbing moans, water pouring over me as I ride it out—grinding into my hand like I can't get enough, like I'm trying to keep him inside me, even if it's only memory.

I feel it everywhere. In my chest. In my toes. Behind my eyes. Like my body is coming apart molecule by molecule.

And when the tremors finally ease, I collapse.

I slide down the wall and let the water rinse the wreckage of me away. My head rests against my knees, my arms limp, my fingers still slick with proof of what I just gave myself. I sit there, chest heaving, legs open, heart pounding hard enough to shake the tile behind me.

And yet I'm still empty.

Because no matter how deep I reached, no matter how hard I came—

What I want is his hands.

His voice in my ear.

His cock fills me up until I forget how to be alone.

Until I forget *how to touch myself,* because no one and I mean no one could ever touch me the way he did.

The water stops, but the heat doesn't leave me.

Steam swirls around my legs as I open the shower door, a warm fog wrapping itself around my calves and thighs like a second skin. I step out slowly, my soles meeting the cool tile floor with a soft slap. The contrast sends a jolt up my spine from hot to cold, wet to air and I suck in a breath.

The air hits my skin in waves, and I feel it everywhere.

Especially there.

Between my legs, the sudden exposure makes me twitch. The slickness of my own arousal, still fresh from the orgasm I pulled out of myself minutes ago, meets the open air and turns sharp. Tingling. Teasing.

It's not just sensitivity, it's the stimulation. Every drop of water sliding from me feels like a slow, deliberate touch. Like fingers tracing my folds. My clit pulses, still swollen, still begging.

And my nipples—God.

They harden instantly as I move into the open. Tight. Diamond-sharp. I glance down and see them peak through the droplets still clinging to my chest they are pink, flushed, *aching*. The cool air licks over them like breath, and I *feel it* all the way down my spine.

I reach for the towel but don't wrap it around myself right away.

Instead, I bring it up slowly, dragging it across my shoulder blades, then down to the small of my back. It's soft, a little scratchy from saltwater and heat, and it scrapes over my skin just enough to make my whole body react.

My nipples brush the towel and I shudder.

It's too much.

But not enough.

I move the towel across my breasts, slow, deliberate strokes that press against those hard, sensitive peaks, and a whimper escapes me before I can stop it. My body arches into the pressure like it's begging to be touched again, really touched. Not by cotton. Not by my own hands.

His.

I lower the towel, trailing it down my belly, and as it reaches the space between my thighs, I hesitate.

There's heat there.

Deep.

A wet, throbbing ache that never really went away.

The air glides against the slickness gathered there, and it lights me up. I tremble not from cold, but from the way even *nothing* can feel like everything when your body's tuned to the right frequency.

I press the towel between my legs, gentle, but it still makes me gasp. I'm sore, stretched, tender in the best way, and the pressure is a reminder of how hard he fucked me. How deep he went. How completely he filled me.

My legs wobble slightly.

I lean against the counter, towel draped loosely around me now, not drying, just touching.

I glance at the mirror.

My skin glows. Damp, flushed, nipples stiff against the terrycloth, my thighs still parted slightly, like I'm expecting someone to step between them.

My lips are parted. My pupils are wide. I look like I've been wrecked. And I have.

By Jorge.

I let the towel slip lower. Let it fall.

My breasts sway with the motion so soft, heavy, exposed and it's too much to look at. And not enough.

I watch myself like I'm not even in my own body. Like I'm outside it. Like I'm him.

Watching me.

Wanting me.

My thighs rub together. There's still slickness there, hot and wet between my legs, and the thought of Jorge stepping into the room and finding me like this—open, flushed, aching—makes me pulse deep inside.

What if he is?

I glance over my shoulder.

Nothing.

But that doesn't stop me.

I bend a little lower, bracing my hands on the edge of the counter, arching my back just slightly, tilting my ass toward the door like I'm offering myself.

Like I want him to take me from behind, right here, towel on the floor, my tits swaying with every thrust.

I imagine his eyes dragging over me. The way he'd grab my hips. The sound he'd make when he sees how wet I already am.

I bring one hand around, between my legs, and stroke once—slow, deep.

I moan.

My head drops forward, forehead brushing the mirror, and my other hand comes up to cup my breast, lifting it, squeezing, thumb circling the tight, aching peak.

I start to move.

Hips rocking gently, small at first. My fingers circle my clit, wet and swollen, and every brush sends a jolt through me. I imagine his voice, rough behind me:

"Touch yourself for me. Let me see how bad you need it."

My breath catches.

I press harder, circling faster, grinding against my hand as my breasts bounce softly with every motion, nipples dragging across my palm, body responding like he's here like he's inside me again.

The image is too real.

I slip two fingers in, gasping, curling them deep. My thighs spread wider, my ass pushing back into nothing, fucking the air like I'm chasing him.

The rhythm builds.

My breath grows ragged. My face twists with it, my jaw slacks, brows drawn, lips parted. I look wild in the mirror. Ferocious. Feral.

My tits bounce with every stroke now, every push of my fingers. I twist one nipple, pinch hard, and my back arches with pleasure.

"Jorge," I whimper. "I'm gonna, fuck I'm gonna come again—"

And I do.

I break.

The orgasm tears through me like lightning, white-hot and shaking. My legs tremble. My hand jerks against my clit, the pressure so sharp I scream, loud, bent over the counter, tits swaying, ass clenched, hips jerking as wave after wave slams into me.

I cry out. His name. My need. My surrender.

It's not sweet. It's not quiet.

It's everything.

When it finally eases, I collapse onto the counter, arms shaking, body soaked in sweat and water and release. My skin is flushed, thighs trembling, chest rising and falling like I've just been fucked within an inch of my life.

And I still want more.

I glance back at the empty doorway again, heart thudding.

If he had walked in—

If he *had* been there—

I don't think I would've survived it.

The mirror is half-fogged from the heat, but I can still see the truth.

My skin is flushed, dewy, lips parted slightly like I've just come up from underwater but I haven't. I've just come apart. Again. My pulse still flutters beneath the surface, a quiet thunder low in my belly, and I can feel the ache between my thighs, slow and deep and not yet settled.

I wipe at the glass absently with my palm and catch the full image of myself: damp skin, tousled hair curling along my collarbones, and nipples that refuse to soften, tight, flushed and aching even under the towel.

I close my eyes and let the memory pulse again.

My hand.

My hips.

The mirror fogging as I bent forward and gave in, face twisted in ecstasy, whispering his name into the steam.

Jorge.

Fuck, I can still feel the echo of it inside me.

I take a breath. Then another.

Eventually, I push off the counter and move back toward the dresser. The towel slides down my hips as I walk, cool air brushing across my freshly touched skin. It's almost overstimulating; especially as it ghosts across the still-sensitive slickness between my legs. The contrast makes me inhale sharply, nipples tightening again as the sensation climbs upward.

Settle, I whisper to my body. But it doesn't listen. It wants *to*.

I choose a black bikini; sleek and snug, not meant to distract but failing anyway. The top clasps behind my back with a quiet snap, lifting and hugging my breasts in a way that only emphasizes how sensitive they still are. The fabric grazes across my nipples and I nearly gasp, the pressure enough to remind me how recently I came.

And how ready I still am to be touched again.

I step into the bottoms and pull them up, the high cut hugging my hips, nestling perfectly into the place where I'm still tender. Still wet. I press the crotch of the suit closer with one slow hand just to settle it and shudder at the contact.

Then I layer on a loose white linen shirt, the sleeves rolled, the buttons done only halfway. It flutters when I move, grazing my thighs, kissing my still-warm skin. I slip into a pair of soft denim cutoffs they are worn in, low-slung. The shorts sit just below my hips, and when I zip them, I feel the pressure right against the most sensitive part of me.

It's good.

It's too good.

I glance down, letting my hands smooth the shirt over my stomach. Beneath the bikini, my nipples are still pebbled. Between my legs, the heat pulses with every step I take.

I grab my dive bag. It's heavy. Necessary. It grounds me in the reality of the day ahead.

But I'm not the same girl who walked into the shower this morning.

Not the anxious new diver.

Not the woman still shaken from last night.

Now, I'm warm.

Thoroughly fucked.

Twice.

And somehow still hungry.

I catch myself in the mirror one last time before I leave the bungalow. My eyes are brighter than they were an hour ago, still half-lidded, still a little dazed but behind them is a kind of focus I didn't have before.

I've tasted something real.

And now I want more.

The sun's already hot when I step outside, the sand is fine and warm beneath my sandals. The breeze smells like salt and hibiscus and a thousand promises. I sling my bag over my shoulder, lift my chin, and walk across the resort toward the dive shop, my hips swaying slightly, every step a secret between my thighs.

If Jorge's down there waiting?

He won't be ready for this.

I pray Jorge looks at me today the way he did last night.

Because I'm not walking away this time.

The dive shop buzzed with midday energy by the time I reached it. Wetsuits dripped from wooden pegs. Buckets of gear clattered against the decking. Tourists gathered in small clusters, faces sun-flushed, voices loud with post-dive excitement.

And there he was.

Jorge stood near the rinse station, towel looped around his neck, his curls still damp from the boat. He was laughing, something low and easy at whatever Lester had just said and even from a distance, I could see the tension was gone from his shoulders. He looked... free. Like someone who'd finally exhaled.

The second his eyes found mine, something shifted in his face. The laugh faded, replaced by something softer, deeper. He smiled. Not polite. Not charming. Real.

My heart jumped. I started toward him—but Lester caught sight of me first.

He tilted his head, a grin spreading slowly across his face as he leaned on the counter.

"Well, well," he said, loud enough to turn a few heads. "Sleeping Beauty returns."

I gave him a withering look. "Morning to you too."

He held up his hands. "Hey, I'm just the messenger. Word travels fast when the boss cancels dives."

That stopped me in my tracks. "He canceled?"

Lester nodded, eyes flicking toward Jorge with a knowing glint. "Afternoon dives. Said he had something 'personal' to handle." He added air quotes for dramatic effect, then leaned closer. "Which is code for: I'd rather be somewhere else with someone I can't stop thinking about."

I tried to hide the way my cheeks flushed. I failed.

Lester's expression softened, the teasing fading into something quieter. "You know he's never done that, right?"

I blinked. "Never?"

"Not once." He paused. "He works. He shows up. Every single day. Storms, breakdowns, hangovers it doesn't matter. The man never bails."

He held my gaze, voice low now. "Until today."

I opened my mouth, but no words came out. I couldn't speak around the sudden thud of my heartbeat. I didn't know what to do with the weight of that choice or how deliberate it was. How loud.

Before I could say anything, Jorge appeared beside me, shoulder brushing mine like it was the most natural thing in the world. He didn't touch me. Not quite. But the proximity was enough to make my whole-body tense with awareness.

"You ready?" he asked, his voice low, meant only for me.

I nodded, still stunned, and we turned together toward the boardwalk, away from the shop, toward the afternoon that suddenly felt like ours.

But we didn't make it far.

A voice, cool and sharp as cracked ice, cut through the salt air like a knife.

"Well, this is cozy."

We both turned.

Laura.

She stood on the edge of the boardwalk, framed by a linen dress that probably cost more than my round-trip flight and a pair of designer sunglasses that reflected nothing but her own smug satisfaction. Her arms were crossed. Her mouth was curved into a smile that wasn't a smile at all.

"Didn't realize the dive staff came with... extracurricular options," she said smoothly, eyes flicking between us like she was reading a script and savoring every cruel line.

My stomach twisted. My chest tightened.

Jorge didn't move. But I felt the energy shift in him; his posture sharpening, shoulders rising like a wall going up brick by brick.

"I suppose when you're on vacation," Laura continued, voice dripping honey, "it's all about indulging. Isn't it?"

My skin burned. My throat went dry. And just like that, I felt the invisible line between us and them—between what this *was* and how it would *look*.

And I knew, in that instant, that the little world we'd built this morning wasn't going to stay untouched.

Not for long.

Chapter 10

Jorge

She was gone.

Not gone like she ran. Not gone like something dramatic. Just… gone.

And somehow, that was worse.

Her absence threaded through my place like wind through palm fronds though subtle, persistent and impossible to ignore. The sheet was still tangled where she'd slept. The porch door was slightly ajar, sea breeze drifting in with the scent of salt and hibiscus and whatever soap she'd used that lingered faintly in the air.

Her coffee mug sat empty on the railing.

She hadn't said goodbye. But then, neither had I.

I'd gotten up before sunrise, slipped out of bed while she was still warm and drowsy and tempting in the worst way. I thought I could keep it light. Going through the motions like this wasn't affecting me. She pulled on my shirt, padded barefoot out onto the porch, leaned into me like she belonged there.

She'd asked me to stay.

I hadn't said no right away.

I'd kissed her. Laughed. Said I had to get to the boat.

Told her I'd be back by noon.

But I didn't stay.

And now she is gone.

I stepped outside and leaned on the same railing she'd touched just hours ago. The morning sun was higher now, casting long shadows over the sand. My shirt still hung over the back of the porch chair still creased from her body, sleeves rolled sloppily like she'd meant to put it on again and changed her mind.

The stupid part of me wanted to pick it up and breathe her in.

I didn't.

I sat down slowly, elbows on knees, and stared out at the water. My place was always quiet, but now it felt like a hollowed-out version of itself. The kind of silence that hums under your skin.

I didn't know what it meant, that she left without a word. Maybe she went to shower. Maybe she needed space. Maybe she didn't want to be here when I got back because she didn't want to face what we were turning into.

And I couldn't blame her.

Because I didn't know how to name it either.

I was good at keeping things clean. No attachments. No entanglements. Guests came and went, and I stayed here, rooted. Reliable. That was the deal.

But Piper had stepped onto my porch like she'd been there a hundred times. Woken up in my bed like it belonged to her too.

And now every part of this house felt off-balance without her in it.

I stood, finally, grabbed my bag and my boots, and made for the path toward the dock. My shoulders were tight. My head full of noise I didn't have the language for.

She was gone.

And I wasn't ready to admit how much that mattered.

The skiff cut clean through the morning glass of the bay, the sun not quite high enough to burn, but already hot on the back of my neck. It was a perfect dive day with clear skies, flat water, and no wind. The kind of morning that usually made everything feel a little lighter.

Not today.

Behind me, Lester unwrapped something with loud, unnecessary crinkling and took a bite that made his jaw snap like he hadn't eaten in weeks.

"You brought a Snickers on the boat?" I asked, not turning around.

"It's breakfast," he said through a mouthful. "It has peanuts."

"You're dripping chocolate on the dive log."

He glanced down, shrugged, and licked a streak off the back of his thumb. "Adds personality."

I didn't respond. I was too busy adjusting the tanks, making sure all the gear was exactly where it needed to be because if I didn't keep my hands busy, I'd start thinking again.

About her.

"You're unusually quiet," Lester added, taking another huge bite and talking through it. "Which, in Jorge-language, means your brain's screaming."

I turned slowly. "Want to guess what happens if you get melted nougat in my regulator?"

"Sexy suffocation?"

I gave him a look. He grinned around the candy bar.

"You were smiling when you showed up this morning," he said. "I'm just saying it's suspicious. You never smile before a dive. Usually, you look like someone stole your last anchor."

I grunted and turned back to the tanks. "Let it go."

"Can't," he said cheerfully. "This is the first time you've shown up looking like you got laid and immediately regretted feeling something about it."

That stopped me cold.

He wasn't wrong. And I hated that he knew it.

But I said nothing. I just finished loading and ran through the dive briefing with the kind of sharp, clipped precision that usually came out when I was trying not to feel anything at all.

We anchored just off the southern reef. Visibility was perfect. A stingray skimmed across the sand near the bow anchor, barely kicking up a cloud. The water was warm. Still.

I guided the dive, gestured to a coral overhang where a sea turtle dozed in the current, answered a few signs, and kept everyone close.

But I wasn't in it.

Not really.

I was still on the porch. Still hearing her voice in my head, soft and teasing. Skip with me. Still remembering the shape of her in my bed and the way she didn't say goodbye.

I surfaced first. Hauled myself onto the skiff and pulled off my mask, blinking against the bright sun. The others were laughing, hauling gear, buzzing from the dive.

Lester climbed up next, dripping and grinning. "Solid dive."

I nodded.

He flopped down on the bench, unzipped his vest, and reached into a dry bag for of course another candy bar. This one a Butterfinger.

"Seriously?" I muttered.

"Stress snack. I'm worried about you."

I gave him a look. "You're worried about your blood sugar."

He broke the bar in half and offered it to me like a peace treaty. I ignored it.

Then, more quietly: "She wasn't there when I got back."

Lester didn't say anything for a moment. Just set the half-eaten bar on the bench beside him and ran a hand through his wet hair.

"You think she's done?"

"I don't know."

"You gonna be okay if she is?"

I didn't answer.

Because no I probably wouldn't be.

The dock was alive with movement. Wetsuits slapped wet against wood. Gear clanked and hissed beneath the rinse station hose. Sunlight shimmered off every surface, sharp enough to sting. The air smelled like salt, neoprene, sunscreen, and the half-spilled protein shake someone had abandoned near the stairs.

Normally, this was my rhythm. My language. Every sound, every motion, familiar and anchoring.

But today, everything felt...off.

I stepped off the boat with my gear slung across one shoulder, jaw tight, stomach empty. The sun was high, hot on the back of my neck. Tourists laughed. Someone called my name.

"Captain Jorge!"

I glanced over. The honeymooner from earlier stood at the edge of the dock, mask dangling around his neck, grinning like we shared some private joke. "That turtle swam right at me! I got it on video do want me to airdrop it?"

"Drop it at the desk," I said without slowing.

He didn't seem to notice I wasn't listening. Most people didn't.

Lester was waiting near the gear shed, towel slung around his neck, holding a bag of bright orange corn puffs like a sacred object. His fingers were stained. He was already chewing.

"You're back," he said, watching me like I might break into song or throw someone off the dock. "You look... haunted. Like you just saw the ghost of a one-night stand with emotional depth."

"Not now."

"Oh, definitely now," he said, following. "I haven't seen you this quiet since that French freediver flirted with you and you forgot how to say 'thank you' in English."

I dropped my gear beside the rinse bins.

"Afternoon dive's full," he added. "Cabin Two, the turtle whisperers, GoPro Girl, and Eel Guy who, for the record, is very pumped about his new laser pointer."

"Cancel it," I said.

Lester froze. One corn puff suspended halfway to his mouth. "What?"

"Cancel the dive. Move them to tomorrow morning. Double stack if we need to."

He blinked. "You're voluntarily canceling... a dive?"

"Yes."

"No equipment failure. No hurricane watch. No one swallowed a jellyfish."

"Nope."

He lowered the corn puff slowly. "Okay. I'm just checking, because last time I asked you to push a dive for boat maintenance, you made me dive with a screwdriver in my BC pocket."

I didn't answer. I just grabbed a towel, wiped the sweat off my neck, and reached for the clipboard.

He stepped in closer. "This is about her, isn't it?"

I didn't have to confirm it. The silence said enough.

Lester nodded like he'd just uncovered a long-lost mystery. "She left."

"She wasn't there when I got back."

"And now you're going after her."

I looked up from the clipboard, met his gaze. "I'm not spending the rest of the day wondering what the hell I didn't say."

He stared at me for a beat, expression unreadable. Then he let out a slow exhale, shaking his head like the world had tilted.

"Man. You really never cancel."

"I did today."

I scratched a firm line across the manifest, ink carving straight through every name.

Behind us, water splashed against the dock. The skiff rocked lazily. A tourist tripped over a coil of rope and blamed the sun.

And then came the voice.

"Hey Jorge?"

Eel Guy.

He emerged from behind the rinse station, clutching his dive log like a Bible, droplets sliding from his still-wet hair onto the laminated cover.

"Quick question. Based on the body length and dorsal fin placement, do you think that moray was *Gymnothorax funebris* or *Gymnothorax moringa*? Because I'm leaning moringa, but there was a lateral ridge that was—"

"Tomorrow," I said flatly.

He hesitated. "Okay, but also, are they monogamous?"

Lester raised a hand. "Stop. Hydrate. Rinse. Go."

Eel Guy looked disappointed but obeyed, muttering about mucus membranes and pair bonding as he wandered away.

Lester turned back to me. "So. You cancel the dive. You leave the shop. You find her. Then what?"

"I say something."

"You *say something,*" he repeated. "Is this like a normal-person 'say something,' or are we talking full-blown, chest-baring, 'you changed me' speech?"

I shook my head. "I don't know."

He studied me for a long moment. Then nodded. "Well. Go. Before I change my mind and make you scrub the tanks instead."

I turned toward the hill and toward the path that curved through the palms and led into town.

I took one step.

Then two.

And stopped.

Because something shifted.

The sound. The energy. The way conversation slowed, lowered, scattered like birds startled from a tree.

Lester caught it too. He tilted his head, looking past me toward the path. His voice dropped an octave.

"Oh... damn."

I turned. And there she was.

Coming down the path like she owned the fucking island.

A loose white shirt open down the middle, fluttering at her sides in the breeze. Just enough movement to catch flashes of the black bikini beneath ,the same one I peeled off her last night like my life depended on it. Her skin glows golden under the sun, legs bare and slicked with heat, and her hair, still damp, clings to the curve of her collarbone like it wants to trace every inch I touched.

She's not walking.

She's gliding.

Slow. Deliberate. Hips rolling in this lazy rhythm like she knows exactly how it looks. And maybe she does. Maybe this is for me. Maybe she *wants* me to see what I did to her. How sore she still is. How her thighs move like something inside her is still echoing me.

Then I see it.

Her nipples are tight, peaked through the thin fabric and barely restrained by the bikini top beneath. Not from the cold. No breeze strong enough to fake that.

That's arousal. Lingering, pulsing, *deliberate.*

My pulse slams against my ribs. My cock throbs behind my board shorts like it wants to break through the seams and walk to her on its own. I shift, subtly, gripping the edge of the counter like it's the only thing keeping me upright.

"Jesus," I mutter under my breath.

"You say something?" Lester's voice cuts in from behind a rack of gear, casual as hell.

I glance over my shoulder, jaw clenched. He's balancing two oxygen tanks on one shoulder and a crate of dive weights in the other like he's auditioning for a CrossFit calendar.

"I said nothing," I grit.

He follows my gaze, then whistles under his breath. "Damn. Morning just got a whole lot better."

"Lester," I snap, low and sharp.

But he just grins like the bastard he is. "Hey man, I'm just saying—if I looked like that walking in, I'd expect a parade. Maybe a slow clap."

He disappears into the gear room, still chuckling, and I barely hear him over the rush of blood in my ears.

She's close now.

Close enough that I can see the way her lips are parted just slightly. The way her breath flutters down her neck. The softness in her eyes.

Or is it danger?

I can't tell.

All I know is, she's walking like she came hard this morning. And not just once. That kind of glow only comes from full-body release, the kind you drag out slowly, the kind that leaves your thighs shaking and your nipples raw from overuse.

And fuck me, I want to ask.

I want to press her against the back wall of the shop, slide my fingers under that bikini and ask her what she thought about when she touched herself. If she touched herself.

But I don't have to ask.

I can see *it.*

She stops a few feet in front of me, the shirt catching on the wind just enough to flutter open and flash the flat plane of her stomach, the edge of her bikini bottoms dipping low over her hips.

It's not a greeting.

It's a threat.

"Afternoon," she says, soft, voice like syrup over heat. Not sweet. Thick. Heavy. Loaded.

I try to speak. Nothing comes out.

Get it together.

"Hey," I say finally, my throat is dry as sand.

I sound like a fucking amateur. Like I didn't spend hours last night with my mouth between her thighs, memorizing the way her breath stutters when she's close.

Lester pops back out of the gear room just in time to save me from drowning. "Y'all need a minute?" he says, eyebrows raised. "I can take a walk. Maybe swim to the next island."

"Lester," I growl.

I don't move.

Because Piper is still staring at me like she *knows*. Like she *feels* what I'm feeling. And I swear to God, if she comes any closer—

I'm going to snap.

She stopped three feet away.

Not close enough to touch, but close enough for the world to narrow. The sound of the waves, the chatter of guests, the buzz of a rinse hose. It all dropped into silence, like someone had turned down the volume on everything that wasn't her.

And still, she didn't look at me right away.

She looked at Lester.

"Hey," she said, voice soft, easy. "You guys looked busy."

Lester opened his mouth. Then he closed it.

Then blinked.

I watched his brain fumble for words like someone had just unplugged and re-plugged his entire nervous system. He wiped his hands on the front of his shirt and said, "We were just... yeah. We were... canceling stuff."

I coughed, trying not to laugh.

Piper gave him a small smile. "Hope I'm not interrupting."

"No!" Lester said, too quickly. "You're... doing the opposite of interrupting. You're... rupting. Enhancing. You're an enhancer."

I shot him a look.

He shrugged, mouthing *I panicked*.

She turned to me next, finally. And when her eyes met mine, it hit harder than I was ready for.

The curve of her mouth was soft, unreadable. Her gaze held steady like she wasn't sure if she should smile or run. Her hair fell over one shoulder, a little wild from the wind, her black bikini top is playing hide and seek with her white shirt showing more every time the wind blows her way...and to make sure I was paying attention every authoritative step she took towards me made her large breasts bounce. The whole sight of her at this moment is doing things to my brain I didn't have the vocabulary for.

But it wasn't just the bikini.

It was her.

Standing in my world like she is the center of it.

I forced myself to breathe. "You clean up nice."

She tilted her head. "So do you. You know...for a guy covered in saltwater and regret."

That made Lester snort.

I kept my eyes on her. "Didn't think I'd see you again today."

"I wasn't sure you wanted to."

"I canceled the dives."

That caught her. Just for a second. Her expression shifted from surprise, to something softer, flickering through her eyes.

Lester looked between us. "I'm just gonna uh—go do something that's not this. Like... wash tanks. Or fall into the ocean."

He backed away like it was his life's mission, arms awkwardly lifting like he didn't know what to do with them. Then he disappeared around the corner of the gear shed, muttering to himself about needing "a snack and maybe a lobotomy."

Now it was just us.

Her, glowing in the afternoon sun.

Me, absolutely undone.

I cleared my throat. "You look…"

"You already said 'nice.' You want to try again?"

I stepped forward, just one pace closer. Not touching. Not yet.

"You look like every reason I wanted to come find you."

And that…*that* was the truth.

She didn't answer right away.

Her eyes stayed on mine, steady, unreadable. A little guarded. A little something else underneath.

Vulnerability?

No. It was deeper than that. Like she was standing at the edge of something with one foot in, one foot out and waiting to see if I'd pull her closer or push her back.

The breeze caught the edge of her shirt and lifted it just slightly, brushing it against her legs. She didn't move. Neither did I.

Finally, she spoke.

"I didn't know if you'd come after me."

"I didn't know if I had a choice."

Her breath caught, just barely. I almost missed it.

She looked down, then back up. "You left."

"I had a boat full of guests."

"You also had me," she said softly. "For a minute."

That landed sharp.

I ran a hand down my face, rough with salt and guilt. "I shouldn't have walked out like that. I was trying to do the responsible thing."

"Responsible sucks," she said, eyes flashing with something brighter. "Just for the record."

I smiled. "Yeah. I figured that out right around the time I realized I couldn't get through the dive without checking the damn dock every five minutes."

That cracked her. Just a little. Her lips twitched. She tried not to smile.

"You're really bad at playing it cool."

"I'm not playing at anything."

Another beat passed between us. The kind that stretches and stretches until one of you either closes it... or walks away.

She shifted her weight, glancing toward the beach path. "I wasn't going to come back here."

"But you did."

"I didn't want to be a complication."

"You're not."

Her brow lifted. "I'm a guest."

"You were never *just* a guest."

She exhaled, the breath catching like she hadn't meant to let it go. Her shoulders relaxed. Just barely.

I took one more step forward. Close enough now that I could smell the soft sweetness of her skin under the sea air. Close enough to see the flicker of doubt still behind her eyes.

"You don't have to stay," I said, quiet. "You don't have to explain anything. But I'm here. If you want me to be."

She blinked up at me.

Then, finally, Piper said the one thing I didn't expect:

"I haven't eaten."

I stared. "That's... okay. That's good. We can eat."

"You're buying," she said, turning, already walking toward the path.

I blinked. "Wait—does that mean...?"

She looked back over her shoulder, a little smirk curving her mouth.

"It means I'm giving you a second chance to get this right. Don't screw it up."

And just like that, she was moving again.

And I was right behind her.

We walked until the resort noise thinned out behind us. Past the beach bars with frozen drinks and techno beats, past the souvenir shops selling seashell wind chimes and ten-dollar sunglasses. The path narrowed, the ground shifting from stone to sand to packed earth.

She didn't ask where we were going. She just followed. Silent. Barefoot. Her red dress catching the breeze, brushing softly against her thighs with every step.

We reached a clearing near the edge of the bay, where the trees parted to reveal a squat, lopsided structure built from weather-worn wood and scraps of tin. A flickering string of mismatched bulbs looped lazily across the awning. One of the chairs outside had three legs. The fourth was a rock. A dog slept beneath it, tail twitching in a dream.

"This," Piper said, pausing beside me, "does not look like it has a cocktail menu."

"Good," I said. "That's how you know the food's legit."

Inside, there were five tables. One old speaker hanging from the rafters crackled with music that might've been bolero. A man behind the counter he was barefoot, gray-haired, shirtless and nodded at me once before disappearing into the back.

We sat at a table near the open wall facing the water. No glass. Just a slatted frame where the sea breeze blew through. A laminated menu, curling at the corners, was clipped to the salt-rusted napkin dispenser.

There were no prices. That meant it was fresh, or it was not available.

"I swear," she said, scanning the page, "I've seen this exact menu in a horror movie."

I smirked. "If we survive, the fried fish will change your life."

A woman emerged from the back barefoot, same as the man, carrying two beers with lime wedges already wedged in the necks. She didn't speak. Just placed them in front of us, nodded once, and left.

The beer was cold. The breeze was warm. And beside me sat a woman who'd once been a stranger, now sitting cross-legged in her red dress, sipping from the bottle like she'd done it a hundred times.

We ate grilled snapper wrapped in banana leaves, plantains crisped in oil, thick-cut fries soaked in lime and chili salt. Her laughter came easier now. Softer. It filled the space like music, like light. The dress no longer stunned me. It was her *being here* that knocked the air from my lungs.

This wasn't dinner. This was something else. Something closer.

She caught me looking.

"What?" she asked, brushing hair out of her face.

I shook my head. "You don't belong here."

Her eyes flicked to mine. "Thanks?"

"I mean that in the best way. This place makes people smaller. You make it bigger."

She went quiet for a second. Then smiled. "You're terrible at compliments."

"Working on it."

She leaned forward, elbows on the table, her bare foot brushing mine under the plastic chair. "Tell me something about you. Something you don't say at the dive shop."

I hesitated. She waited.

"I never bring people here," I said finally.

"Why?"

"Because this place doesn't try to be anything it's not. And I like it that way."

She smiled, slow and knowing. "And you brought me."

"Yeah."

Another pause.

"You know I'm leaving soon," she said quietly.

"I know."

"But you're still here."

"I'm still here."

She looked down at her beer. Then back up at me.

"So now what?"

I didn't have an answer.

But I was already trying to imagine one.

The sun had slipped behind the waterline, casting the sky in layers of bruised lavender and rose-gold. The string lights above our table buzzed faintly to life, flickering like fireflies caught in salt air. A breeze lifted off the water, soft and balmy, curling strands of Piper's hair against her cheek.

She laughed at something I said, easy and open, her hand wrapped around the neck of a half-empty beer bottle, her bare foot brushing mine under the table like it had the right to be there.

And maybe it did.

For the first time all day, it felt like we weren't counting down. Like the clock had stopped.

Her painted-on shorts, those goddamn long legs, had settled into the shadows like something made for twilight the deep red, soft at the edges, and molded to her body in a way that made it impossible to look away.

This woman. On this island. At my table.

If I let myself think about it too long, I'd start believing it was real.

"Okay," she said, leaning forward, a grin playing at her lips, "but I still want the dive story. Your first one. No edits."

I groaned. "I told you, it's terrible."

"All the better."

I smiled. I couldn't help it. "Twelve years old. I slipped trying to get into the boat, scraped my leg wide open on the ladder. Spent the entire dive convinced I was bleeding out and going to be eaten alive."

Her mouth dropped open, laughing. "That's not just terrible, that's tragic."

I was about to respond with something smart, something soft when the air around us shifted.

A drop in pressure. A subtle hush. Like the bar had inhaled all at once and forgot how to exhale.

And then—

"Well. This is unexpected."

The voice landed like a cold hand to the back of my neck.

Smooth. Confident. A little too pleased with itself.

I didn't need to turn.

I already knew.

Mark.

He strolled into the warm spill of string lights like he'd just walked off the cover of some travel magazine. Linen shirt. Tan. Sunglasses still tucked into the collar like he hadn't noticed the sun was gone. He walked like he owned the whole damn island.

My spine straightened.

Piper turned slowly, her smile fading just enough to register.

"Didn't peg this as your kind of place, Jorge," Mark said as he approached, hands casually in his pockets. "You finally expanding your horizons?"

I didn't respond.

Because I was watching her.

Her posture had changed not dramatically, but enough. Her shoulders lifted slightly. Her hand left the bottle. Her gaze sharpened.

And when Mark's eyes landed on her, that smirk deepened.

"Well, *damn*," he said, eyes lighting up like he was seeing something valuable. "Piper."

My jaw clenched.

And then she said it.

"Hi, Mark."

Two words.

Soft. Controlled.

And somehow the most painful thing I'd heard all day.

Not *Who are you?* Not *Do I know you?*

But *hi*.

Like they'd met before.

Like she *knew* him.

Like this wasn't the first time he'd said her name like that.

Mark glanced at me, just a flick of the eyes, then back to her. He gestured to the empty chair beside her with a casual confidence that made my stomach turn.

"You mind if I sit?"

He was already pulling the chair back.

Piper didn't answer.

Neither did I.

Because whatever this was about to become—it had just changed.

Chapter 11

Piper

He says my name like he still owns it.

"Piper."

Two syllables. Too familiar.

And just like that, the night tilts off balance.

The sound cuts clean through the quiet between me and Jorge with the low hum of music, the soft scrape of waves against the shore, the easy warmth of his foot nudging mine beneath the table. It all vanishes, like someone's pulled the thread and unraveled the moment in a single, practiced tug.

I know that voice. That tone. The way it wraps around a room like it was always meant to be the center of attention.

I turn, and there he is.

Mark.

Crisp linen shirt. Tan that's too perfect to be real. That same smile the wide, calculated, and a little too proud of itself. He steps forward with the confidence of a man who's never been told no and never learned how to stay gone.

He looks right at me as he slides a chair back from our table.

Uninvited.

Unbothered.

And suddenly, it's like I'm back in every room I've ever tried to leave. Every conversation where I smiled too long. Laughed too much. I made myself small just to keep the peace.

Mark hasn't changed.

And for one awful second, I wonder if I have.

Because my throat is tight, and my grip on the beer bottle is too firm, and I can't seem to pull my eyes away from him.

Worse—Jorge hasn't said a word.

I glance sideways.

He's still.

Focused.

Waiting.

And the silence between us feels louder than anything Mark could say.

My pulse kicks up. The skin on my chest prickles. That warm, open, golden feeling I had ten seconds ago while sharing fries, teasing stories, thinking maybe this could be something—slips through my fingers like sand.

Because now I'm not sure what this is.

And the question rises, hot and sharp in the back of my mind:

Am I just a fling?

Just a girl Jorge brought to dinner before he sent her back to the airport.

Mark smiles wider, sensing the shift. He looks between us like he's doing the math, and I hate how calm he looks. How easy it all is for him.

He sits.

And no one stops him.

I stay perfectly still.

My shoulders don't move. My face doesn't twitch. I lift the bottle, sip from it slowly, and nod at something no one has said.

But inside?

I'm unraveling.

My mind is racing through a thousand versions of this moment, rewinding, recalculating, redrawing every interaction Jorge and I have had over the past few days. Every glance. Every kiss. Every soft thing he murmured with his lips pressed against my skin.

And now I can't tell if any of it was real.

Because he's sitting beside me like a statue. Not protective. Not proud. Just quiet.

Just there.

And it shouldn't matter. I should be strong enough to hold myself upright. I should be able to look at Mark, laugh in his face, and let it bounce off me like it's nothing.

But it isn't nothing.

It's him. Jorge.

He's the one I let in. The one I didn't expect to want. The one I didn't plan on trusting, but somehow did anyway.

And now, sitting in the space between Mark's attention and Jorge's silence, I feel exposed in a way I haven't in years. Naked, but not in the fun, tangled-in-his-sheets kind of way. More like; peeled open. Every nerve humming with the memory of what it feels like to be almost enough.

I hate how quickly it takes me here.

How fast I start running down that old, familiar hallway.

I was too much. Too eager. Too *hopeful*.

I'm the girl who falls in love on vacation, gets her heart stomped at the gate, and pretends she's fine when she walks back onto the plane.

And wasn't that exactly what I promised myself I wouldn't do this time?

I came here to *escape* all that. To breathe. To stop giving my heart away to people who weren't holding out their hands in the first place.

But Jorge... God, he made me believe he was different. Not with big declarations or grand gestures. But in a quiet way. The way he looked at me when he thought I wasn't paying attention. The way he remembered how I liked my eggs. The way his whole body stilled when I touched him.

Now?

Now he's staring at Mark like he's trying to measure something. Like *I'm the thing on the scale.*

And all I can think is:

Don't leave me out here alone.

Not again.

Mark smiles like this is casual. Like this isn't a needle he's slipping just under the skin.

"You know," he says, leaning back in his chair, "when I saw you at the resort bar that first night, I thought you looked familiar. But I couldn't quite place it."

My breath stutters in my chest.

He's bluffing. That's what I want to believe. Just another one of his little games. But his voice is too calm, too sure, too *casually rehearsed*.

Then he tilts his head, eyes narrowing slightly, like it just came to him.

"White dress," he says. "Sitting by the window. You were sketching something on a napkin. Dock lights, maybe? It looked like you knew the place."

My stomach drops.

He's right.

God—he's exactly right.

That was my first night here. Alone. Tired. Trying to breathe through a delayed flight and a panic spiral and the sudden, stupid hope that a change of scenery might change something in *me*. I remember sitting at that bar, ordering a rum drink with too much sugar and not enough alcohol. I remember putting my headphones in. I remember ignoring everyone around me.

I don't remember him.

But clearly, he remembered *me*.

I force myself to stay still, though every cell in my body wants to move. To run. To throw this chair through the nearest wall.

"I didn't think much of it," he continues, his tone so relaxed it almost passes as kind. "Until I saw you with him. Then it all clicked."

He doesn't gesture. He doesn't need to.

His gaze slides from me to Jorge and back again, dragging that invisible implication like a net between us.

Small island.

Big mistake.

And I feel it, *I feel it* the moment Jorge shifts beside me.

It's subtle. A breath caught too long. A muscle drawn tight. But I know his body now. I've mapped it with my hands, with my mouth. I know the difference between his stillness and his tension. And this?

This is a man pulling back.

My vision narrows.

Mark takes a slow sip of his beer, like this is the most natural conversation in the world. Like he's done us both a favor by mentioning it.

But I know what he just did.

He didn't just drag up a harmless memory.

He cast a shadow.

He laid out a timeline and stepped back, letting it twist itself into something ugly.

He made me look like someone who flirts in bars and slips away before the name matters. Like someone who's already done this once this week, maybe twice. Like someone who's *playing* Jorge.

And Jorge is still silent and lets the moment hang.

That silence?

It cuts.

It lands harder than any accusation Mark could've made.

Because now it feels like Jorge is processing it. Turning it over. Questioning what he thought he knew.

And I can't stop thinking:

He didn't even ask me.

Not even a glance. Not even a quiet, did that happen? or What is he talking about?

Just silence.

Just doubts.

Just distance blooming like frost between us.

I want to speak. To explain. To snap back at Mark and tell him I don't owe him anything. That the only mistake I made was not walking out of that bar five minutes sooner.

But I can't tell which man I'd be explaining it to.

And suddenly, I feel so exposed.

Not because of what happened that night.

But because I let myself believe this meant more.

And now I'm watching the moment it starts to come undone.

And I feel it the moment Jorge shifts beside me.

It's subtle. A breath caught too long. A muscle drawn tight. But I know his body now. I've mapped it with my hands, with my mouth. I know the difference between his stillness and his tension. And this?

This is a man holding the line.

Jorge's voice is low and measured when it finally breaks the silence.

"You've said enough, Mark."

Mark leans in slightly, tone still breezy. "Relax. Just catching up with an old friend."

"You don't have friends," Jorge says flatly. "You have clients. Tourists you upsell and reef guides you plagiarize."

Mark smirks, but it wavers. Jorge isn't done.

"And for the record—you didn't see her. You watched her."

That lands like a shot.

And he's not looking at Mark when he says it.

He's looking at *me*.

Like those words were only ever meant for me to hear.

And something about that, about the way his eyes stay steady, about the quiet claim beneath the calm—undoes me.

Mark exhales like he's bored. "No need to get territorial."

"Then maybe don't sniff around what's not yours," Jorge replies, voice low and precise.

Mark flinches. Barely. But I see it.

And then Jorge delivers the final blow.

"Oh—and one more thing," he says. "If you're going to sneak around the resort trying to poach my clients, maybe don't do it where the staff can hear you."

Mark freezes, just for a beat.

Jorge leans back, like the point has been made. Like the conversation is already over.

"And next time," he adds, "don't use her as your excuse to get close."

The silence that follows is deadly.

Mark straightens, smoothing a hand over the front of his shirt like he needs something to do.

"Well," he mutters, trying to keep the heat from rising, "you always did take things a little too personally."

Jorge's voice is quiet. Final.

"Only when it matters."

And that's it.

Mark doesn't argue. Doesn't throw a parting shot.

He just walks away.

Mark disappears into the dark, swallowed by the curve of the path and the sound of the sea. The hum of the restaurant drifts back in like background noise—clinking glasses, laughter from another table, the soft thump of music leaking from the kitchen.

But our table?

It's silent.

Tense.

Radiating heat like the air hasn't cooled at all.

I look at Jorge.

He's still watching the spot where Mark vanished. His jaw is clenched, shoulders stiff beneath the worn cotton of his shirt, one hand curled so tightly around his beer bottle I half expect it to shatter.

But when he finally turns to me, his expression is *nothing* like I expect.

No anger.

No bravado.

Just... something stripped bare.

"I can't—" He stops, exhales hard. Tries again. "I can't do this if you think I'm like him."

The words hit harder than I'm ready for.

My chest tightens.

"I don't," I say quickly, quietly. "Jorge, I don't—"

But he's already shaking his head. "It's not just about tonight. It's not just Mark. It's..." He presses his fingers to his temple like he's trying to organize the wildfire behind his eyes. "I've never done this before."

He looks at me then like really looks at me and my whole body goes still.

"I've never let someone in like this. Not since I came here. Not since I built this life with my name on the sign and my head down and my rules written in stone."

He swallows hard. His throat works like it costs him something.

"And then you show up," he says, voice rough. "And you laugh at my silence and touch me like I matter and make me think about things I've spent *years* trying not to want."

My heart is in my throat.

He's not performing.

He's not protecting anything.

He's just *telling me the truth*.

"I didn't plan for you," he says, softer now. "But I'd be lying if I said I haven't thought about what happens when you leave. And it scares the hell out of me."

My breath catches.

I want to reach for him. Say something. Anything. But I don't move.

Because he's not done.

"I don't know what this is," he says. "But it's real for me."

And then, without waiting for my reply, Jorge stands.

He takes the beer bottle with him, walks around the table, past the string lights and the flickering shadows and the people who have no idea what just cracked open in the middle of this place.

I turn to watch him go, heart pounding like it's trying to catch up with his feet.

He heads toward the beach, not in anger, not to retreat but to breathe. To feel the sand under his feet and the sea air in his lungs.

To *stand still* before he does something reckless.

He stops just at the edge of the surf, bottle in one hand, shoulders back, staring out at the horizon like it has answers.

And all I can do is sit there, stunned.

Wanting to follow.

Terrified to move.

And wondering if maybe—just maybe I've been looking at the wrong kind of bravery this whole time.

He stands there like a statue, legs planted in the sand, staring out at the horizon like the answers might be out there somewhere, buried in the dark water or folded into the stars.

I watch the breeze lift the edge of his shirt. Watch the tension ripple across his shoulders.

And still... he doesn't move.

So, I do.

I stand, legs shaky beneath me, and step down from the restaurant's warmth into the cool weight of the night. The sand is soft and cold under my feet. The wind hits me like a whisper. It's warm and salted and thick with everything we're not saying.

I walk to him. Slowly. Each step is deliberate. Not chasing. Not pleading.

Choosing.

The moon lights the water in silver ribbons, and for a second, we're just two shadows in the dark.

He hears me coming. I know he does.

But he doesn't turn.

So, I stop beside him. Close, but not touching. Letting the space speak for itself.

"I'm not going to let you walk away from what you just said."

My voice is calm. Too calm. Because inside I am spinning. Every nerve is alive. Every breath is shallow. But I hold steady.

He doesn't respond. Doesn't even flinch.

"You don't get to say those things and then stare at the ocean like they were nothing," I add. "You don't get to hand me the truth and then pretend like you didn't mean it."

His jaw shifts. Just barely. But it's the first sign he's still in there, somewhere beneath the silence.

"I'm still here," I say, softer now. "Even after all that. I'm standing right here. And if you think that's easy for me, if you think this doesn't scare the hell out of me too then you don't know me at all."

That gets him.

He turns his head, eyes finding mine in the dark. And what I see there is not indifference. It's not guilt.

It's fear.

But not of me.

Of *everything else.*

"I meant it," he says, voice low, raw. "Every word."

"I know."

"But?" I ask, because I can see it in his eyes. The hesitation. The pull.

He looks down at our feet, buried in the sand. Shakes his head once, like he's trying to shake loose a thought that won't let go.

"I don't know how to want something like this and not break it," he says. "Not ruin it. Not ruin *you.*"

The words hit somewhere deep.

Because I've been broken before. And ruined. And I've blamed myself for all of it.

But somehow, this man, the one who holds himself together with silence and seawater and stubbornness thinks *he's* the danger.

"I'm not asking you to be perfect," I whisper. "I'm not asking you to promise anything you can't give."

I take a slow step forward, so close now I can feel the heat of him, the tremble under his stillness.

"I'm just asking you to *try*."

He closes his eyes, breathing hard like the tide inside him is rising too fast.

"I don't know if I'm built for this," he says. "I've spent so long keeping my head down, staying safe, staying in control. You show up and suddenly none of it works the way it used to."

I reach for his hand.

I wrap my fingers around his, slowly, gently, until he lets go of the bottle, he's still holding like it's the only solid thing left.

It falls into the sand with a soft thunk.

"I don't want the version of you that's always in control," I say, voice barely above the sound of the waves. "I want *this one*. The one standing here. Shaking. Trying."

He looks at me like I just gave him something he didn't know he needed.

Or something he doesn't think he deserves.

"I'm scared," he says, so quietly I almost miss it.

I step in, closing the last inch of space between us.

"So am I," I whisper. "But I'm still here."

His breath stumbles.

And then, finally, his hands wrap around mine—tight, warm, grounding.

Not perfect.

Not steady.

But *real.*

He doesn't kiss me.

He doesn't say he loves me.

He just holds on like he's afraid to let go.

And for now... that's everything.

Jorge's hands are wrapped around mine, not with desperation or demand, but with quiet certainty as though he's holding something he never expected to deserve, and is still figuring out how not to break it.

For the first time since the moment Mark walked in, I feel something steady settle beneath my ribs. Not peace exactly, but a fragile version of it. A breath I didn't know I was holding. A center I didn't think I'd find tonight.

We're not touching like lovers. We're not saying things like promises. But there's something alive in the space between us now, something tender and trembling, built not on impulse but on honesty. I can feel it; this beginning, this risk and for a second, I let myself believe in it. In him. In us.

And then my phone vibrates against my leg.

The sound is soft, nearly lost beneath the hush of the tide and the wind curling off the sea, but it slices clean through the moment like a sudden change in current.

I hesitate, wishing I could ignore it.

But muscle memory takes over. My hand moves without permission, reaching for the device I thought I'd forgotten. I glance at the screen, just to make sure it's not something serious, some vague emergency from back home I didn't know I was waiting for.

It's not.

But somehow—it is.

Olivia: Hey, just a reminder—your lease ends next week. Are you still planning to renew, or should I take it? Let me know ASAP. We need to give notice.

That's all.

No exclamation point. No emojis. Just a clean, unfeeling tether to a life that suddenly feels galaxies away from the sand beneath my feet and the man in front of me who just opened himself up in a way I *know* cost him something.

Still, it lands with the force of a gut punch.

Because it's not just about the lease.

It's about the apartment I never loved but never left. It's about the job I didn't plan to quit. The city I told myself I still belonged to. The version of me that lives there, who plays it safe and plans everything and says no when something feels too good to last. The version I swore I'd come back to after this trip, unchanged. Unshaken.

But now?

Now I'm standing barefoot in the sand, heart still trembling from the way Jorge said *this is real*, and I don't know how to fit that woman and this moment into the same life.

I reread the message like the words might rearrange themselves into something easier, something less final. But they don't.

They stay crisp and cool and utterly indifferent to the swell of feeling sitting in my throat.

I look up at Jorge, who's still holding my hands, still watching me with that searching expression that makes it so hard to lie.

And for the first time tonight, I don't know what to do with the truth.

Because the part of me that was brave enough to walk toward him is now wrestling with the part that remembers how to leave before it hurts too much to go.

And in this suspended second I'm caught between the life I built and the one I never meant to fall into and I feel everything tightening again.

The tide is rising.

And I don't know if I'm about to swim or run.

Chapter 12

Jorge

I got to the dive shop earlier than usual, hoping the salt in the air would scrub my head clean.

It didn't.

The sun hadn't even cleared the edge of the dock when I unlocked the gear shed and stepped into the soft clatter of tanks shifting in the shadows. Everything looked the same the masks stacked, fins drying, boat lines coiled in neat, practiced loops. It was familiar. Predictable. The kind of order I used to depend on.

But none of it felt grounding today.

I was still spinning from the night before, still holding onto the weight of her hands in mine, the truth I spilled without filters, and the look in her eyes when her phone lit up with that text. That one reminder of everything waiting for her elsewhere.

I didn't sleep much. Didn't eat. Just replayed every second in my head until even the silence between us started sounding like something I'd said wrong.

Lester was already behind the desk when I walked in, hunched over his third breakfast of the morning with a bag of plantain chips and a can of something fizzy and neon-orange.

He looked up, squinting like I was a ghost. "You're alive."

I grunted, dragging out the clipboard and flipping through the dive log.

He crunched a chip. "How's the brooding? Still at a healthy smolder, or are we approaching full tortured-heart territory?"

I didn't answer.

Mostly because I didn't have one that didn't sound like I wanted to hit something.

"Right," he muttered. "Full tortured-heart it is."

A few guests trickled in the usual mix of wide-eyed first-timers and over-prepared returners. I gave them the morning briefing, told them we were doubling back on yesterday's canceled dive, promised reef walls and nurse sharks and better visibility than the charts predicted. My voice did what it always did. Calm. Controlled. Like I hadn't cracked open less than twelve hours ago.

When they were gone, Lester was still watching me.

"You're gonna pretend nothing happened?" he asked.

I shot him a warning look.

He ignored it.

"She stayed," he said. "That's not nothing."

"She got a message."

"I figured. She looked rattled when she walked past the porch."

"It was about her lease. From someone back home. Reality knocking on her door."

Lester frowned, slower this time. "You think she's already halfway gone?"

"I think she's still standing on the beach with one foot in the water and the other pointed toward the airport."

He didn't say anything for a second.

Lester tossed the empty chip bag into the bin and wiped his hands on his board shorts like that counted as hygiene. "You know he's been creeping around the resort all week, right?"

I looked up. "Mark?"

"Yeah, Mark. Mr. Look-at-my-synthetic-wet-suit-and-say-it's-custom. I saw him lurking near the juice bar yesterday morning, chatting up GoPro Girl and the honeymooners. Offered them a free night dive. Said it was part of a *'collaboration package.'*"

I stared at him.

"He's poaching."

Lester snorted. "He's always poaching. It's in his DNA. But this time? This wasn't business. This was personal."

I said nothing.

He took that as permission to keep going. "You don't think it's weird he magically showed up at the one place you *never* bring guests? That he sat down like he owned the table? That he just happened to know Piper's name?"

I clenched my jaw.

"I mean, I wouldn't put it past him to dig through a guest roster or bribe a concierge just to sniff around your personal life. You know how he is and can't stand the idea that someone else has something he wants. Especially if he didn't get it first."

I exhaled through my nose, slow and sharp. "You think he knew about us?"

"I think he knew enough to make it uncomfortable. And I think he saw you walking into that restaurant with your armor down and thought, *'Finally. A soft target.'*"

I didn't answer.

Mostly because I was still feeling the weight of those five seconds when Mark looked at Piper like she was a story he already knew and how quickly I started wondering if he was right.

Lester leaned his elbows on the counter and studied me. "He wasn't there for her. Not really. He was there for you."

I looked up.

"He saw something in your face," he said, quieter now. "Something he could shake loose."

And just like that, everything from last night echoed back—her hands in mine, the words I almost didn't say, the way she looked down at her phone like it was a map pulling her somewhere I couldn't follow.

Mark saw it too.

And now, he'd sunk his hook.

The dock creaked underfoot as I made one last pass around the boat. Everything was prepped—regulators checked, tanks lined up, BCDs inflated and ready, gear bags stowed neatly along the port rail. The motor hummed low in the background, a steady thrum I usually found comforting. Today it just felt like noise.

The dive group was almost fully assembled, chatting in scattered pockets of excitement. One of the honeymooners was triple-checking her GoPro mount like it was a NASA payload. Another guest was already halfway into his wetsuit, asking if we'd see reef sharks today like he was requesting a song.

I answered on autopilot. I smiled when I needed to. I nodded where appropriate. My hands worked like they always did steady, practiced and unflinching but everything inside me felt tight, like my chest hadn't fully loosened since last night.

Lester stood just off the dock ramp, leaning against the cooler like it was a throne and he was some kind of snack-smeared king. He had on that faded rash guard that said *Dive Hard* in peeling white letters and held a can of mango soda in one hand like a morning trophy.

"You look like you're trying not to think," he said, deadpan.

I didn't respond.

He took a long sip and squinted toward the end of the dock. "How's that working out for you?"

Still nothing from me.

Because I'd already counted ten guests. And we had a spot for eleven.

And even though I'd told myself not to hope and not to *expect*, I couldn't stop my eyes from flicking toward the shoreline every few minutes like some idiot dog waiting at a window.

She hadn't said she'd come.

She hadn't said she wouldn't.

All she'd done was look at me like she was already slipping away.

The sun had climbed higher while we loaded up, the sky turning that wide, impossible blue that always made the water look deeper. The wind had calmed. The tide had started to push in. Everything about the day screamed perfect.

Except me.

Except this ache I couldn't name, sitting just beneath my ribs like pressure that hadn't equalized.

Then I heard footsteps.

Slow, purposeful. A rhythm that didn't match the hurried clatter of fins or the slap of gear bags. A softer sound, Certain.

I turned toward it, already knowing.

And there she was.

Piper.

She walked toward us like she had all the time in the world. No mask of ease, no apology for being the last to arrive, just that quiet, centered way she had when she was trying not to show how much it cost her to show up at all.

Her hair was pulled back in a loose knot. She wore a simple black swimsuit under a dive skin that hugged her curves like it was designed for her alone. Her towel was slung over one shoulder, her mask clipped to her hip, her steps slow but deliberate.

She didn't look like someone running away.

She looked like someone walking toward a decision.

And for one suspended second, I forgot how to move.

She didn't search the crowd. Didn't scan for approval or hover awkwardly at the edge like she didn't belong. She just walked right down the dock toward the boat, toward me and when our eyes met, I felt something shift in the air between us.

Not a full smile. Not quite a relief.

But something.

A nod.

A flicker of recognition.

A silent *I'm here.*

And somehow, it was enough.

My shoulders dropped half an inch. The breath I hadn't realized I was holding slid out of my chest like a slow tide pulling back from shore.

Lester saw her too, his eyebrows rising just enough to count.

He leaned in toward me, voice pitched low and dry. "Well, well. Looks like our eleventh diver made the call after all."

I didn't look at him.

Didn't need to.

Because I was already watching her step onto the boat like she wasn't the reason I'd lost sleep and found something too close to hope.

And for the first time since last night, I didn't feel like I was waiting for the other shoe to drop.

I just felt like I wanted to know what came next.

The deck of the boat vibrated with energy the fins slapped against the hull, zippers hissed shut, and laughter bounced off the water like it had somewhere better to be. It was the kind of organized chaos I usually found grounding. But this morning? It felt like a noise in my chest.

I moved through the motions, checking gear, adjusting tanks, giving half-answers that still passed for confidence. My hands were steady. My voice is professional. But inside, everything felt just a little off-axis. Like a current was pushing against me I couldn't see.

Piper was already aboard she was quiet, efficient, unreadable. She'd taken the seat near the stern ladder, clipped her mask to her side, and said little more than good morning. No eye contact. No softness. Just a calm, cool presence. The same one I'd admired a hundred times. The same one I suddenly wasn't sure I had the right to reach for anymore.

She was here.

But she was *drifting*.

"Today is the day!" Rahn beamed, his grin wide and contagious as he unwrapped a protein bar with one hand and loaded his gear with the other. "Reef wall, baby. I can feel it in my spine that it's gonna be magic."

Laura, hunched over her camera rig, didn't look up. "Just don't kick up silt again like yesterday."

"I was excited!" Rahn protested, laughing. "I got carried away! The reef forgave me. I made peace with a grouper, I swear."

"Was that before or after you nearly crashed into the fan coral?" Chuck cut in, already halfway into his wetsuit. His tone, clipped and superior, landed like a cold splash. "There's a reason we follow the plan."

Rahn just grinned at him, completely unaffected. "You're right, Chuck. Next time, I'll send the coral an apology bouquet."

Laura snorted. "Get it waterproofed."

I was about to step in when Lester strolled across the deck wearing his rash guard emblazoned with a neon seahorse and carrying a half-eaten bag of cheese puffs. How he managed to eat snacks this close to descent time was beyond me.

"Alright, my undersea adventurers," he called out, voice full of mock ceremony. "Let's honor the sacred tradition of keeping your fins out of my damn face, and we'll all survive the morning."

"Don't listen to him," Rahn said cheerfully. "He's just mad because the fish never follow him."

"I once had a parrotfish ignore me for an entire dive," Lester replied, pointing at him with a puff-dusted finger. "That's emotional damage I'm still processing."

While the boat buzzed around me, I kept one ear tuned to the conversation happening just a few feet from where I stood.

Matt.

The solo diver. Keen-eyed. Quiet. Always on the edge of the group, but watching everything.

He was seated beside Piper, adjusting the straps on his gear. I watched him lean over, voice low and measured.

"You seem different today," he said.

Piper glanced at him, slow and deliberate. "Do I?"

"Yeah. Not in a bad way. Just… quieter. Pulled back."

She didn't answer right away.

Matt continued, more careful now. "You're becoming a solo, you know. It's not about diving alone, it's about pulling your focus inward. There's a shift. I've seen it. Felt it myself."

Piper looked away, out toward the water. "Maybe I just needed space."

"Or maybe," Matt said gently, "you're figuring out who you are without everyone else's noise."

I felt the weight of it like a sudden drop in temperature. The way he said it. The way she didn't argue.

She was slipping.

Becoming her own island in a group she'd only just started to belong to.

Lester, standing beside me now, leaned in. "You okay?"

"I'm fine," I said, sharper than I meant to.

He raised an eyebrow. "Yeah. That's convincing."

I cleared my throat and called out, "Buddy checks! Let's make sure no one's descending without a tank, yeah?"

Chuck stood immediately, correcting Rahn's strap like he was preparing for a polo match.

Laura double-checked her camera housing.

Rahn bounced on his heels like a kid waiting for recess.

Piper moved last, quiet and precise, her eyes scanning her gear like it was a checklist she could hide behind.

"Dive plan's simple," I said, stepping up to the rail. "We'll start on the reef slope, descend to twenty meters, drift with the current, and loop back along the wall. Stay with your partner, don't touch the coral, and if you see a moray eel Matt, I'm looking at you, don't propose to it."

Laughter rippled across the deck.

Even Piper smiled just barely.

I caught it, held onto it for a second longer than I should've.

Then I nodded. "Let's get in."

Rahn whooped and jumped first, splashing with wild, joyful abandon.

Laura followed with practiced grace, GoPro already blinking.

Chuck adjusted his mask like it was a designer accessory before sliding in with smooth precision.

Matt moved to the rail and turned to Piper. "See you down there."

She gave him a small nod, then stepped forward.

She looked at me.

One second.

Maybe two.

And whatever was in her eyes, I still couldn't name it.

Then she was gone, sliding beneath the water like she belonged there more than she ever had on land.

And I was left with the sound of my own breath.

The water wrapped around us like silk and silence, everything slowing down the second I sank beneath the surface. The reef bloomed below in bright greens and soft purples, fanned out like an invitation but my chest stayed tight, lungs never quite filling the way they should.

Usually, the descent cleared my head. Usually, I find peace here.

But today, the stillness only amplified what was already unraveling.

Piper moved just ahead of the group, a clean line of motion in the water. It was calm, composed, precise. Her buoyancy was perfect. Her trim textbook. But there was a distance to her movements that didn't come from depth, it came from something deeper. Something heavier.

She wasn't diving with us.

She was *diving near* us.

Matt kept close—too close, in a way that didn't break protocol but still registered. I could see the flicker of recognition in his movements, the way he matched her pace but gave her room, like someone who knew what it felt like to need space, but not *isolation*.

I hovered nearby, watching as Rahn veered enthusiastically toward a cluster of garden eels and threw two shaka signs in opposite directions like he'd just discovered the secret to life. The eels disappeared instantly, but Rahn seemed to take it as a spiritual triumph.

Lester floated just beneath him, perfectly horizontal, arms crossed and motionless like he was judging the reef itself. He rolled slowly into an upside-down hover in front of a coral shelf and mimed applause for no one but himself.

Laura, camera always rolling, drifted smoothly over a bed of feather stars while Chuck lingered behind her, gesturing for her to stay *just* out of his shot, though I wasn't sure if he meant the footage or his life.

And through it all Piper drifted like a shadow at the edge of it all. No buddy contact. No shared signals. Her world reduced to her fins, her mask, and the reef beneath her. A perfect solo trim. A perfect solo silence.

And I hated it.

Not because it broke any rule but because I used to be part of that stillness with her.

Now, I wasn't even a ripple.

Matt passed by again and gave her a gentle OK sign. She returned it without hesitation but didn't make eye contact. Just floated, distant and self-contained.

I caught his eye as he turned. It wasn't smug. It wasn't possessive.

It was understanding.

He was watching her drift the same way I was like she was halfway into another current. And neither of us knew if she'd come back.

I checked on the group, signaled the route forward with two fingers and a sweep of my hand, and we moved along the reef edge in pairs and trios. Matt gave me a slight nod as he fell back.

Rahn hovered near a crevice, dramatically signaling "big" with both hands and then tossing another double shaka toward a passing grouper who did not share his enthusiasm and swam off like it had better things to do.

Even the fish were avoiding us.

I drifted closer to Piper as she paused near a large coral head. She didn't look over, didn't signal. Just stayed there, floating still, hands resting lightly by her BCD, eyes fixed on the slow undulation of a fan coral.

She didn't need help. She didn't need me.

And that was the worst part.

When it was time to begin our ascent, I gave the upward signal, slowly and deliberately, then checked each diver in turn. Everyone responded. Everyone rose.

Piper followed last.

Still silent.

Still alone.

And as I kicked upward beside her, I realized the deeper pressure hadn't come from the ocean at all.

It had come from the space she'd left behind.

The boat rocked gently under the late morning sun, hull creaking just enough to remind us we were still at sea, still floating, still between worlds.

Divers peeled off gear with the sluggish ease of post-dive bliss with wetsuits half-down, salt in their hair, faces flushed and glowing. The deck smelled like neoprene, sunscreen, and ocean.

The surface interval was always a strange limbo: too short for real rest, too long to ignore your thoughts.

I moved among them, checking air levels and logging bottom times, but mostly trying to keep my eyes off Piper.

She was near the stern, sitting on the rail with her legs swinging over the water, hair damp and wind-tangled, sipping from a water bottle Lester had tossed her without a word. She wasn't avoiding me, but she wasn't inviting anything either. Just... there. Quiet. Calm. Edges hard to read.

Rahn flopped beside her, still dripping and grinning like he'd just won a prize.

"That grouper hated me," he announced proudly.

Piper glanced over; eyebrows raised. "You were throwing shakas at it."

"It was a peace offering."

"It looked terrified."

"Nah," Rahn said. "It just wasn't ready for my energy."

That got a real smile out of her, small, but honest. A flicker of something warm I hadn't seen since before the dive. She nudged him with her shoulder. "Maybe next time lead with a dance."

Rahn gasped, hand to chest. "Underwater interpretive eel ballet. I've been *training for this moment.*"

Chuck, seated under the canopy and drying his hands with a towel he somehow made look expensive, scoffed. "You two treat every dive like it's a circus. There's a reason instructors emphasize discipline."

"You're right, Chuck," Rahn said solemnly. "Next time I'll file a TPS report before smiling at a fish."

Laura, hunched over her GoPro on the opposite bench, didn't look up. "Your bubbles photobombed my octopus shot."

"Worth it," Rahn said, unapologetic.

Lester appeared with two energy bars and one half-open soda. "I'll trade one of these for a guarantee no one swims through the fan coral on the next drop."

"Can I bribe the ocean not to push me into it?" Piper asked.

"Nope," Lester replied. "That's part of the rite of passage. One brush with coral doom, and then you're spiritually certified."

Matt sat nearby, silent until now. He was peeling back his wetsuit sleeve and drying his hands slowly with a towel as he looked at me.

When he spoke, it was low. Measured. "She's good. Controlled. But she's drifting."

I looked at him. "I noticed."

"You gonna let her?"

It wasn't a challenge.

It was worse.

It was an honest question.

I didn't answer. Just stood there too long and looked out over the water, pretending the sun was too bright to squint through. Pretending the ache in my jaw was from the salt.

Matt didn't push. He just nodded and went back to his water bottle like he hadn't just said something that cracked me open a little further.

Lester clapped his hands. "Alright, my salty seahorses! Next dives in thirty minutes. Hydrate or I will personally yeet your fins into the current."

"You can't use 'yeet' after forty," Laura mumbled, still watching her GoPro screen.

"I'm twenty-nine in *reef years,*" Lester replied without missing a beat.

Rahn raised his arms like a preacher. "Praise the reef!"

Chuck groaned. "Please."

But I barely heard them.

Because across the boat, Piper was laughing.

Soft.

Real.

And not for me.

Not yet.

But something told me that she might still be reachable.

If I could figure out how to reach her without pushing her further out to sea.

I stood near the bow and let the sea breeze sweep across my face before turning back to the group, raising my voice just enough to cut through the scattered hum of chatter and gear clicks.

"Alright, next dive." I glanced down at the log slate, though I didn't need to. "We're headed south, along the ridge drop. The current's light viz looks great, and we've got the entire back wall to ourselves."

That got a few murmurs of appreciation. Laura perked up, already turning her GoPro rig toward the rail, as if prepping her lens for greatness.

"We'll descend at the mooring line," I continued, pacing slowly as eyes turned toward me. "Drop to eighteen meters, skirt the slope until we hit the swim-through. Keep your trim tight through the arch there's a fan cluster halfway in. On the other side, we'll loop back with the drift."

Rahn clapped his hands once, eager. "Sharks?"

I shrugged. "Maybe."

"Ray sightings?" Laura asked, more businesslike.

"Two earlier," I said. "Could be more."

"Can we summon them?" Rahn said, eyes wide with faux seriousness. "Do I need to chant?"

"If you do," Lester called from the cooler, "do it overboard."

"Ancient reef incantations," Rahn muttered to Piper, who actually smiled, just a little. "Totally real. Very effective."

Chuck sighed, like we were all beneath him. "If everyone could refrain from trying to *manifest marine life,* that'd be great. This is a dive site, not a cruise talent show."

Lester, unbothered, raised his can in salute. "Speak for yourself. My interpretive sea cucumber routine deserves an audience."

Laura just groaned and rolled her eyes, muttering, "I *knew* I should've booked the Tuesday slot."

Despite myself, I felt the edge in my chest loosen. A little.

I looked over at Piper. She was half-geared already, adjusting her rigging with the practiced calm of someone trying to disappear into motion—but I caught it; the soft glance she threw Rahn's way, the way her body angled toward the group this time instead of away. Less float, more anchor.

I didn't let myself linger.

"Checks in five," I said. "We dive in ten. Hydrate. Equalize early. And for the love of the reef, don't touch the damn coral."

"Do *not* summon the octopus," Lester added gravely. "He's still mad about Rahn."

"Hey!" Rahn shouted. "That octopus *liked* me."

"Sure," Laura said. "He *inked* you."

"Love comes in many forms."

The ocean swallowed us again but this time, it felt different.

The drop was smooth, practiced. Sunlight knifed through the surface like golden silk, scattering across the divers below like stardust. The ridge rose gently from the seafloor, then curved away into deeper blue like it was leading us somewhere ancient.

This part of the reef was quieter, older. Sponges bloomed in deep orange along the slope; their ridges curled like open mouths. Fish scattered in slow-motion flashes of blue tangs, striped grunts, a pair of angelfish that moved like they didn't care who we were or why we were there.

Piper hovered just ahead of me, her form precise, stillness carved in water. She wasn't leading this time but she wasn't on the edges either. She stayed near the center of the group, her fin kicks slow, controlled. Her hands hung loose by her BCD; fingers relaxed.

She wasn't *reachable*. Not yet.

But she was *present*.

And that after the last two days felt like something.

I gave her a wide berth, drifting alongside Rahn and Laura as we moved past a shallow coral bloom. Rahn spotted a passing ray and did a full body wave dance in response, flaring his arms like seaweed and tossing a double shaka at the sky. The ray flicked away, unimpressed.

Even the ocean had boundaries.

Lester, predictably, found the largest sea cucumber he could and spent a full minute miming a dramatic monologue to it while Matt hovered nearby, watching Piper not creepily, just... attentively. Like he saw something shifting in her the way divers notice changing currents.

And maybe he did.

Because she *was* shifting.

She paused beside the swim-through and looked back not at Matt. Not at the reef. At me.

Just for a second.

And it wasn't an apology.

It wasn't a question.

It was something smaller. Quieter. Like the beginning of permission.

I nodded—small, steady.

And she moved forward.

We swam beneath the coral arch, our silhouettes stretching long
across the reef floor. On the other side, the current picked up,
carrying us slow and easy across soft mounds of sand and scattered bommies teeming with cleaner wrasse and sleepy squir-
relfish.

Rahn turned his body into a lazy barrel roll, spinning through
a column of bubbles like a show-off seal pup, and Laura filmed
him while muttering "idiot" into her regulator. Chuck stayed
dead center, finning mechanically, probably calculating his air
to the breath.

Piper stayed close.

And when we began our ascent, her hand brushed past mine as
we kicked upward.

Barely a touch.

Maybe an accident.

But maybe not.

We rose in staggered pairs, bubbles breaking toward the sky in
slow, spiraling threads. The water narrowed around us as the
sun reached down, arms of gold pulling us back toward air,
toward noise, toward whatever came next.

And for the first time in two days—

I surfaced with hope.

The boat bumped gently against the dock as Lester tossed the line and tied us off like he was doing it in a dream. The sun hung lower now, casting long golden streaks across the planks and lighting up the surface of the water in broken glass patterns.

The group was loose-limbed and flushed from the second dive, the sun-warm and ocean-heavy in that way only divers know. Wetsuits peeled down, hair plastered with salt, everyone glowing with that quiet buzz of having touched something deep and come back whole.

Rahn jumped to the dock first, twisting midair with a whoop like he'd just dismounted from the Olympics. "Ten out of ten. Would descend again."

"You *almost* took out the mooring line," Laura muttered, stepping off behind him. "Graceful as a cannonball."

Lester followed, dragging a cooler behind him and announcing to no one, "I'm claiming the hammock tonight. Whoever steals it gets cursed by the reef gods and me personally."

Chuck stepped off like the dock was trying to trick him, smoothing his shirt immediately and already pulling out his phone, which he hadn't touched in three hours and seemed desperate to reattach to his soul.

Matt helped pass up the last tank before slinging his bag over his shoulder and walking past me with a nod. "Good dive."

"Yeah," I said, then added, "Thanks for keeping an eye out."

He paused mid-step. "She's not lost, you know."

Then he walked on.

I watched him go, heat rising in my chest for reasons I didn't fully understand.

Piper climbed up last, barefoot, damp hair twisted over one shoulder, face flushed. She didn't look at me. But she didn't rush past either. Just stepped onto the dock like she was still deciding where she stood.

I turned to face the group.

"Hey," I called out. They slowed, half-turning, grinning, already halfway gone in their own post-dive highs. "Tonight—a bonfire at the south beach. Just past the fishing dock. Bring drinks, bring stories, bring whatever you want. It'll start at sundown. Anyone's welcome."

Rahn raised his arms to the sky. "YES. Fire. Ocean. S'mores. LET'S GOOOOO."

Lester fist-pumped with his bag of snacks. "I'm bringing a portable speaker and absolutely no taste in music."

Laura looked interested. Chuck looked annoyed. Matt said nothing, but nodded once. Rahn was already trying to organize some kind of driftwood dance circle.

And Piper she just looked right at me, Not long. Not intense. But enough.

Her eyes held something I couldn't name. Not warmth. Not rejection. Just... something suspended.

Before I could step closer, I heard it.

A soft voice, just behind her.

Laura, hushed, casual. "Are you going?"

Piper hesitated, tucking a loose strand of hair behind her ear.

"I don't know," she said.

And that was it.

But those three words?

They landed harder than anything else that day.

Chapter 13

Jorge

By the time I got the fire going, the sky looked like Bob Ross had risen from the dead, poured himself a rum punch, and gone absolutely feral with a brush.

Colors bled into each other like the clouds had feelings in deep coral near the horizon, melting into gold, into plum, into the kind of indigo you only get when the night wants to make you ache. The light kissed the surf, soft and molten, and stretched long shadows across the curve of the beach.

It was the kind of evening that made people believe in staying. Or at least in never wanting to leave.

Lester was barefoot and shirtless, wearing a linen button-up open to his navel, spinning in lazy circles as he checked the speaker setup he'd dragged down in a cooler earlier. A warm blend of Caribbean steel drums and acoustic guitar drifted out into the salt air, the beat low and slow, laid back but alive, like the island itself was stretching into the night.

I added another piece of driftwood to the flames and stepped back, watching the fire settle into a wide, steady burn. The heat licked at my shins. Sparks popped once, then again, rising into the dusk like stars in a hurry.

I wiped my palms on my shorts and tried not to look at the path.

"She'll come," Lester said behind me, not turning from the speaker.

I didn't answer. Just adjusted the logs and stared into the orange.

People started to arrive in slow pairs, some barefoot, some with beach towels over their shoulders, some already glowing with sun and rum.

Chuck and Laura were first, carrying their own folding chairs and matching expressions of skepticism. Chuck immediately asked if the food was catered. It wasn't.

Rahn came next, holding a six-pack of some obscure tropical soda and wearing a shirt with pineapples, parrots, and something questionable smoking a cigar.

"Fire looks righteous," he said, setting the sodas near the coolers. "Let's summon the reef gods and get weird."

Matt walked up beside Jack, who nodded at me with that same easy steadiness he always carried like he was older than the sea, and twice as patient. He set down a cooler and gestured toward the fire.

"Caught 'em an hour ago," he said. "Wrapped in salt and banana leaf. We'll lay 'em in once the flames go low."

"Appreciate you, Jack," I said.

He gave a small nod, like words weren't worth wasting on things already understood.

The fire crackled. The music floated higher, a soft marimba weaving through the chords. Someone laughed. Someone cracked open a beer. Nina came down from the path with her camera swinging at her side, already snapping candid shots in the firelight.

The group was forming.

The beach is alive.

And still she wasn't here.

The sky turned deeper, inkier. The stars began to blink through, shy and sharp.

I fed the fire again.

And waited.

The party had found its rhythm.

Jack had the fish laid out in foil over a bed of coals, the skin crisping with that perfect mix of smoke and salt. Someone, most likely Rahn, had started mixing rum punch in a washed-out cooler, and it was dangerously good. Too sweet, too easy, and already responsible for two of Chuck's louder-than-necessary opinions.

Lester had built a circle out of mismatched cushions and driftwood benches, and people took turns flopping down, drinks in hand, sun in their hair. The music had shifted into slower grooves now the steel pan easing into nylon-string guitar, soft vocals in patois floating over the breeze like a lullaby you could sway to.

Stories bloomed.

Rahn, half sprawled on a towel, launched into one of his signature tales. "Remember that eel cave I swore was clear? I got stuck in the *entrance, my mask* full of sand, fins flapping like a cat in a sink. I thought I was gonna die. Chuck had to yank me out like a cork."

"You're welcome," Chuck said, mostly to himself, already halfway into his second drink.

Laura passed around her GoPro, showing off the moment the sea turtle had passed right by her shoulder. "He looked at me like I was interrupting something extremely important," she said. "Which, fair."

Jack chuckled from the grill. "Turtles always look like they know secrets they're not telling."

People laughed. The fire cracked louder. Someone passed a bottle of dark rum around the circle, and the flames caught it just right, reflecting deep amber off glass and eyes alike. The stars began to thicken above, clear and sharp, as if the island sky wanted in on the story, too.

And I, I tried.

I smiled. I laughed at the right parts. I passed drinks and nodded along and even threw in a story of my own about a dive gone sideways with a manta ray that apparently had a grudge against fins.

But all the while, I kept glancing toward the path.

Still nothing.

I'd told myself I wouldn't be obvious. That I wouldn't scan the beach like some love-sick idiot hoping for a miracle dressed in linen and moonlight.

But I was.

And just then she arrived.

Piper stepped into the edge of the firelight like the night had saved its breath just for her.

Barefoot. Wrapped in a two-piece floral set that looked like it had been painted on by the gods of temptation themselves with a strapless tube top that clung in all the right ways and a matching flowy skirt that shifted like petals with every breeze. Her skin was sun-warmed and glowing, freckled across her collarbones and shoulders, kissed by salt and dusk. Hair down, wind-tousled and wild, catching bits of firelight like gold dust. She looked like she'd just come from seducing the tide.

Every conversation died for half a beat.

Or maybe it just did in my chest.

She didn't rush. Didn't fidget. Just walked toward the fire with her head high, her eyes steady. She didn't look at me.

Not yet.

But I could feel her.

Like gravity had picked a side.

Piper

The first step onto the sand nearly undid me.

Warm, soft, whispering between my toes. The fire ahead cast long shadows across the beach, dancing over driftwood and bodies sprawled in lazy, rum-fueled comfort. Music swelled low and rich—steel drums curling through the air like smoke, a rhythm that felt like a heartbeat half-remembered.

It should've been intimidating, all those people laughing and glowing in the firelight. But it wasn't.

It felt like walking into a dream.

And he was there. Jorge. Sitting near the flames, one hand wrapped around a drink, the other resting on his knee like he wasn't holding back the urge to get up. His profile was lit in gold, sharp and devastating. He looked like something carved out of the night, waiting for something or someone.

Me.

I felt every eye find me. Conversations stumbled. A hush without a reason.

But in an instant Rahn was suddenly in front of me, arms open, half-drunk and glowing with joy.

"Piper!" he said like we were lifelong friends reunited in a movie montage. "You *made it*! I was starting to bet you were a mirage!"

I laughed, grateful for the buffer. "It would've been a lot weirder if I showed up riding a dolphin."

"Oh my god, don't *threaten me* with a good time," he said, taking my hand and spinning me dramatically toward the fire. "Come. You need some punch. Possibly food. Definitely both."

I caught Jorge's eyes just over Rahn's shoulder.

Something flickered there.

But before I could make a move, Rahn was guiding me toward the drink cooler, still narrating my entrance like I was Cinderella at the ball and he was my personal island hype man.

Chuck offered me a half-hearted nod from his chair. Laura lifted her GoPro in a silent toast. Jack just smiled from the grill like he already knew how this story ended.

I wanted to go to Jorge.

But the party wrapped around me fast from arms to laughter, glasses offered and stories retold. It was warm. Loud. Easy.

And just for a little longer, I let myself float in it.

Just long enough to feel him watching.

Just long enough to pretend I hadn't come here just for him.

The first drink tasted like a mistake; it was sweet, fizzy, and sneaky as hell. The second? That one had rhythm. It smoothed out the edges. Let me settle onto a driftwood bench with bare legs curled up beneath me while the firelight warmed one side of my face and the ocean wind cooled the other.

Matt slid into the open spot beside me like he belonged there. "Glad you came," he said, easy and honest.

"Me too," I said, and I meant it.

He handed me a grilled skewer from Jack's stash without asking. Fish, pineapple, something spicy-sweet on the edges. Perfect. We ate in companionable silence for a few minutes while Chuck launched into a half-sober lecture about nitrogen narcosis and how he'd once navigated a wreck blindfolded to prove a point. No one asked what the point was.

Jack shook his head. "If a man ever tells you he dove blindfolded for fun, check his air mix."

"Or his ego," Matt added, raising his cup.

Lester plopped down next to me and leaned in like he was about to share a state secret. "Just so you know, this rum punch is approximately seventy percent rum and thirty percent decisions you'll regret by midnight."

"Sounds like a challenge," I said.

"I love that about you," he replied, grinning wide. "But also, hydrate. Because I will not be holding anyone's hair later, no matter how emotionally invested I am."

We all laughed. And something loosened in my chest.

The third drink made me bolder. Not reckless. But aware of my skin, my smile, the way the firelight curved over the edges of my thighs. I felt the beat of the music in my ribs now, like a second pulse. The air buzzed with salt and possibility.

I caught Jorge's eyes again across the fire. Just for a breath. Just long enough.

He was looking at me like he remembered every second of the other night.

And like it was killing him not to cross the flames.

Then someone handed me another drink, and the music shifted yet again faster now, full of hand drums and clapping. A rhythm that felt like running downhill barefoot. I let the fire and the people carry me, laughter caught in my throat, warm on my cheeks.

But he was still there.

Burning steady across the flames.

At some point, I drifted. Not far but just enough to breathe. The music, the warmth, the buzz of too many drinks was perfect, but I needed a second alone. I wandered down the beach toward the darker edge of the cove, where the firelight gave way to shadows and the water whispered its secrets just for me.

The sky was full now. Stars spilled across it like someone had scattered diamonds over velvet. I tipped my head back and let the moment settle, heavy and light all at once. My pulse was still elevated, my skin still humming, but the air out here was cooler, quieter. Honest.

A breeze tugged at the hem of my skirt. I curled my arms around myself, not from the chill, but from the sudden weight of everything.

And then, from behind me—

"Careful. That's how the sea seduces you. Whispering like that. You'll start naming the waves and end up eloping with a tide pool."

I turned.

Lester.

He was holding two coconuts, both with tiny umbrellas and mismatched straws. "I brought backup hydration. I may be tipsy, but I'm also a hero."

I laughed, genuinely, as I took one. "You're the weirdest guardian angel I've ever had."

He plopped down beside me in a puff of sand, cross-legged, the hem of his linen pants already soaked at the cuffs. His shirt was open enough to qualify as suggestive or oblivious but knowing Lester, probably both.

"You know," he said, sipping with dramatic flair, "in my unofficial professional opinion, you're dangerously close to the 'late-night emotional revelation' portion of the bonfire."

"Am I?" I said, raising an eyebrow.

He nodded solemnly. "It starts with stargazing. Then comes the confession. Then the kissing, then the regrets. Or not. Honestly, it's a crapshoot."

I rolled my eyes. "You really have a chart for this, don't you?"

"I *am* the chart."

We both laughed again. The kind of laugh that released something. He quieted after a moment, swirling his drink.

"I've seen a lot of people come through this island," he said. "Some run toward something. Some run away. Some fall in love with the island, some fall in love with each other. And some"—he glanced over at me "fall in love with themselves for the first time."

I didn't answer right away.

He looked back out toward the water. "You're in the tricky category. You're still writing your ending."

"Which category is Jorge in?"

Lester exhaled, slow. "He's the chapter people don't expect. The one that either changes the whole damn book or breaks your heart beautifully."

My smile faltered, but not from fear. From recognition.

He bumped his shoulder into mine. "But hey. I'm just the comic relief."

I raised my coconut. "To comic reliefs who say the truth when no one else will."

He tapped his drink against mine. "To brave girls in floral skirts and big feelings."

We drank. We watched the stars. And in that quiet curve of sand, where no one was asking anything of me, I felt more myself than I had in weeks.

Not Jorge's maybe. Not the resort guest. Not the woman everyone saw walking out of the firelight like she owned the world.

Just Piper.

And just for a split second that felt like enough.

Jorge

I saw them before I even heard them, these two shadows returning to the edge of the firelight, laughter soft and private like something precious.

Lester, of course, ridiculous as ever, balancing a coconut drink like it was a royal goblet. And Piper, God Piper.

Barefoot in the sand, her long legs kissed golden by the firelight, smooth and strong with the kind of confidence that made your throat dry. The skirt of her floral set danced around her thighs, teasing glimpses of toned muscle and sun-warmed skin. Her stomach was bare and flat, soft in the glow, the kind of curve that made you ache to touch without ruining it. And that top; strapless, snug, showing off the slope of her collarbones, the soft swell of her breasts catching the light like they belonged in a damn painting. It was unreal. She was unreal.

Her hair fell in waves around her shoulders, wild from the sea breeze, shining like it had stolen its color from the fire. She didn't just walk. She glided. Like the tide made way for her. Like gravity had realigned to watch her move.

Her laugh was low but full, a little slurred with rum—melted through the night like sugar on heat. She didn't even try to be perfect. She just *was*. Effortless. Sensual. Powerful in the kind of way that made a man forget how to stand still.

And I?

I couldn't look away.

She brushed her hair behind one ear with her free hand, and even that small motion felt choreographed by the gods. The kind of thing you don't forget, even years from now when you're doing something stupid like washing dishes and suddenly your chest caves in with the memory.

Lester said something that made her snort-laugh, and she playfully shoved his shoulder. He spun dramatically like he'd been mortally wounded, then bowed low as he handed her off to the firelight, like she was royalty and he'd simply escorted her to the edge of the ballroom.

And she paused.

Just long enough to find me.

Her eyes locked on mine.

This time, she didn't look away.

And then slowly, carefully, like the moment deserved reverence.She started to walk toward me.

Every step was a thunderclap in my chest.

Like the earth shifted to make room for her.

My lungs forgot their purpose. My heartbeat stuttered like it couldn't keep pace with the sight of her. I was rooted and floating all at once, the way you are in a dream that feels too real to be safe. It was that slow-motion, high school movie moment—the one where the lights dim, the bass drops out, and suddenly you're the only one who knows something extraordinary is about to happen.

And the hottest girl in the universe? She's walking toward *you*.

The fire flickered around her like it knew what was coming, casting gold and orange halos over the swell of her breasts, the dip of her waist, the sinuous lines of her legs. Her skirt shifted with each step like petals brushing her thighs, and her hips rolled with the kind of rhythm that made time lose count.

The world narrowed. Rahn's laugh, Chuck's smug commentary, even Lester's latest one-liner all of it dropped into a hush. The only sound that mattered was the soft thud of her bare feet in the sand and the beat of my own heart trying to leap from my chest.

She held her coconut drink like it was just an accessory to the curve of her wrist. Her other hand hung loose by her side, grazing the fabric at her hip. Then she lifted her eyes through thick eyelashes with those bright, dark, wicked eyes and smiled.

Not a grin. Not a polite, party-smile.

A knowing smile. One that said she knew exactly what she looked like. Knew exactly what she did to me.

It hit me in the gut. Lit a fuse down my spine.

I felt seventeen and thirty-seven at the same time—awkward and desperate and high off adrenaline, like if I blinked, she might vanish. Like I'd somehow been gifted this impossible, beautiful girl and all I could do was hope I didn't screw it up.

I was seconds from combusting.

When she was only a few feet away but close enough that I could see the shimmer of salt still clinging to her collarbone, the firelight catching in the strands of her hair I stood.

My legs moved on instinct. My words didn't dare.

She stopped in front of me. The air between us pulsed.

Her eyes searched mine, burning with a question I was ready to answer.

And then she said, soft as sin—

"Hey."

And it was over. One simple word, I was hers.

Piper

He stood so fast it nearly knocked the breath out of me. Jorge. Towering in the firelight, jaw tight, eyes locked on me like I was some cosmic event he didn't want to miss. I could feel his gaze on every inch of my skin, like it burned its own kind of warmth into me.

"Hey," I said, barely more than a breath, because my throat had forgotten how to speak around him.

His mouth parted like he wanted to answer, but no words came. There was only that intensity: it was hot, focused, magnetic.

So, I closed the space between us.

One step. Then another.

Close enough to smell him the salt and driftwood and something warm, something man. His shirt was open just enough at the top for me to see the thick line of muscle that carved down his neck into his chest, and the sleeves were rolled to his elbows, revealing forearms that looked built for holding, for anchoring. His hands hung tense at his sides like he didn't know what to do with them now that I was here.

My eyes trailed lower. His cargo shorts sat low on narrow hips, and I could see the outline of his thigh through the fabric, taut from standing too still. The firelight cast shadows in the lines of his abs beneath the thin cotton of his shirt, and I was suddenly, acutely aware of how close we were.

"You've been staring at me all night," I murmured, voice silk and challenging. My hair slid over my shoulder as I tilted my head, brushing against my bare skin like a slow tease.

His throat worked as he swallowed. "You make it hard not to."

I smiled, let it be slow and wicked. I took a sip of my drink, letting the straw glide between my lips, drawing it out. His eyes followed every movement like he was starved. When I licked a bit of rum from the corner of my mouth, I watched the heat spike behind his gaze.

"Dangerous to look at me like that," I said, licking my bottom lip.

"You want me to stop?"

I stepped closer, our bodies brushing now, soft fabric against hot skin. His breath caught, and so did mine. The space between us disappeared.

"I didn't say that."

The fire crackled behind us, casting a warm orange glow over his skin. I tipped my chin up, letting my eyes drag over every inch of him from his sculpted shoulders, his throat with that slight shadow of stubble, the sharp angle of his jawline that looked like it could cut steel.

His hands twitched, like he was holding himself back. Like touching me would ruin the tension we'd built. But I didn't want restraint. I wanted the slow, unbearable pull of him unraveling.

"You know," I said, my voice barely a whisper, just for him, "if you're going to keep looking at me like that... you should probably do something about it."

His jaw flexed again, that telltale sign he was feeling everything and trying not to lose it.

I smiled—no, I smirked because *now* the power had shifted.

And I liked how it felt.

"Or," I added, taking one small step forward, letting my lips hover just inches from his, "I could keep talking until you can't take it anymore."

His breath brushed my cheek. He hadn't moved.

But something in him had snapped.

And I was ready for what came next.

Jorge

But we never got the chance to find out.

Not yet.

Because the party, as if on cue, began to dissolve around us.

Someone laughed too loudly behind me Rahn, probably he was everywhere tonight and half cut, followed by the unmistakable thump of a cooler lid being slammed shut and the shuffling of feet on sand. The music dipped lower, voices turned to murmurs, and the firelight stretched longer shadows across the beach as people began drifting away in pairs or stumbling solo toward the paths.

I blinked just in time to catch Laura stretching like a cat, arms overhead, her GoPro dangling from one wrist. "I need sleep before the next dive," she mumbled, already turning away. Chuck hovered behind her, watching Piper like she was a puzzle he couldn't quite solve. He gave me a tight nod as they passed—respect, or indigestion. Could've gone either way. Laura offered Piper a slow, knowing glance and shot me a wink I didn't acknowledge.

Piper stepped back. Just half an inch.

But I felt it like a gust of cold air under my skin.

People started saying their goodbyes. The spell of the night, all boozy and sun-drenched, full of music and fire slowly began to unspool thread by thread.

Matt lingered by the embers, trading a low word with Jack. Jack gave him one of those subtle, grounded nods that said more than a conversation. Then Matt looked my way, lifted his chin. "Bonfire's done, man. But something tells me the real fire just started."

I didn't respond. I couldn't. I was too busy watching her.

Piper tucked a strand of hair behind her ear, cheeks still flushed maybe from the rum, maybe from something hotter. Her lips were parted, soft and shining, and her eyes sparkled under the fading light like they held secrets the stars couldn't keep. Her skin glowed in that firelit way that felt unreal, like the gods had leaned in a little too close when they made her.

Rahn staggered by holding a half-empty soda bottle like a trophy. "You two gonna make out now or do I have to come back and narrate it?"

Before I could react, Lester materialized and looped an arm around Rahn's shoulders like he was scooping a toddler out of a minefield. "Don't ruin it! Let the tension marinate, for god's sake."

Piper laughed. A soft, breathy sound that shattered me in the gentlest way.

I looked at her again and really looked.

Her hair was wind-tossed and wild, framing her face in unruly waves that made her look like she belonged to the ocean. Her lips were still damp from her drink, and her body had gone loose in that late-night, sun-soaked, rum-heavy kind of way that made every movement look like an invitation. The way she shifted her weight from foot to foot, bare toes curling in the sand, the glint of firelight against her skin it was all too much and not enough.

She looked like the end of the night and the beginning of every mistake I wanted to make twice.

The beach cleared like a slow tide pulling back. Jack gathered up the last of the food, humming under his breath. Laura's GoPro light blinked off in the trees. Even the music had stopped now, leaving only the soft pulse of the waves and the crackle of the fire, low and steady.

And then it was just us.

The silence was full. Charged. Every inch of space between us is humming like a live wire.

I turned to her fully, the fire casting flickers across her collarbone and down the slope of her chest.

"I thought you weren't coming tonight," I said, my voice lower than I meant, like I was already halfway into a confession.

She looked up at me, the corner of her mouth tilting, eyes bright with something unreadable like hesitation, heat mixed with hope.

"I almost didn't," she said, voice as soft as the breeze off the water.

And just like that, the moment cracked open.

Because now the fire wasn't behind us it was *between* us.

It danced in every glance, every breath, every inch of space we hadn't closed yet.

And I didn't want to wait any longer.

Not one more breath.

She's standing in front of me, framed by firelight.

One leg slightly bent, shirt hanging off one shoulder, skin glowing, lips parted. The flames behind her flicker and twist like they're drawn to her body, the curve of her waist, the outline of her breasts beneath thin cotton, the glint of sweat along her collarbone.

I can't move.

Can't breathe.

The air between us isn't just charged, it's *primed*. Like the moment before lightning hits the earth.

She looks over her shoulder at me, eyes wide, heat simmering low in them. Her breath's shallow. Her mouth opens, but she doesn't speak.

She doesn't have to.

She knows what she's doing. She knows what I've been holding back. She knows I'm two seconds from losing it.

And I do.

I close the space between us in three long strides. One hand slid into her hair, the other grips her hip, and I press myself flush to her back. She gasps it's soft and sharp as my mouth finds the side of her neck, teeth scraping just enough to make her shiver.

"You have no idea what you're doing to me," I growl against her skin.

"Then show me," she whispers.

Fuck.

I spin her around, fast, and she lands against the wall beside the fire her eyes wide, lips parted, chest rising fast beneath the cling of that half-unbuttoned shirt. The flicker of flame dances across her skin, painting her in heat and shadow, and I swear she's the most beautiful thing I've ever seen.

"You sure?" I ask, one last time.

She nods, slow and sure. "I want all of it."

I kiss her like I'm starving. Tongue deep. Teeth clashing. My hands slide beneath her shirt, up her back, and I pull the fabric off her shoulders, let it fall to the floor.

Her bikini top is still on just barely. I slide one finger beneath the strap and snap it loose. It falls between us. Her breasts are flushed, nipples tight, begging to be touched and I do. I palm one, thumb circling slowly, watching the way her lips part, the sound that escapes her.

I drop to my knees and kiss her stomach, her hips, the soft flesh between her thighs. I hook my thumbs into her bikini bottoms and drag them down inch by inch, my mouth chasing every patch of newly bared skin. By the time I reach her knees, she's trembling.

Still standing.

Still watching me.

Still holding on to the last edge of control.

Not for long.

I rise again, chest to hers, cock straining in my shorts as I kiss her like I want to crawl inside her soul. My hand slides between her thighs and I feel she's wet, hot, *ready*. She gasps into my mouth as I stroke her slowly, and her hips roll against my hand like her body's already saying yes.

Then she does it.

She reaches between us.

Her fingers slide down, slow and certain, and tug my waistband down just enough to slip her hand inside. When she wraps her fingers around my cock it's skin to skin, heat to heat I can't help but groan, deep and guttural, forehead falling to hers.

"Let me," she whispers.

And I let her.

She pulls me out, her grip confident, her touch reverent. Stroking me once slowly, purposefully before guiding me between her thighs.

I reach down, line myself up.

And just as the fire flares behind her I push inside.

I push into her slowly, and the second I feel her stretch around me she's tight, hot, soaked to the fucking core every muscle in my body clenches.

She gasps, her back arching against the wall, and her eyes flutter shut. Her lips part on a sound so soft, so raw, it nearly floors me.

I stop.

I just *breathe.*

Because being inside her? It's not just good.

It's goddamn holy.

Like her body was made to take mine. Like all the noise in my head, the years of restraint, the ache I didn't know I was carrying, *this* is the cure.

I stay buried deep, chest to chest, my hand gripping her thigh as I hold her up. She's trembling already, her breath hitching, her nails biting into my shoulders like she's hanging on to reality by a thread.

"Fuck," I groan, my voice wrecked. "You feel..."

She looks at me, pupils blown wide. "*Jorge.*"

That's all she says.

But that's everything.

I pull back, slow, almost to the tip, and then thrust back in fast and *deep*. And her whole-body jolts. Her head drops back, mouth open, moaning my name again, and it's the sound I didn't know I needed to live.

I set a rhythm. *Slow. Deep. Intentional.*

Each stroke drags through her like a promise. Each thrust lands with a groan, a gasp, a whispered fuck from one of us.

She holds me tighter, wrapping her legs around my waist, pulling me impossibly close. Her breasts press against my chest, soft and slick with sweat, her nipples hard as glass against my skin. I kiss her almost sloppy and definitely hungry, gasping between thrusts and I feel her body start to roll with mine.

"You want it slow?" I whisper, lips brushing hers. "Or hard?"

She doesn't flinch.

Her voice is breathless, wrecked, *commanding*. "Both."

My control shatters.

I slam into her once, hard enough to knock the air from both of us. She chokes on a gasp, legs tightening around me, and that noise *the noise* that drives me fucking wild.

I grab her ass, lifting her higher against the wall, and *fuck* her. Raw. Deep. Hungry.

The room echoes with skin slapping, with wet, filthy sounds of our bodies colliding. The fire behind her throws gold across her skin, her stomach flexing, her throat exposed, her hair sticking to her cheeks as she moans like she's unraveling.

"You're perfect like this," I groan against her neck, my hips snapping into hers. "*Perfect.* You love it when I fuck you like this, don't you?"

She nods, whimpering. "Yes...*yes* harder don't stop *please*—"

I pull back to watch her face, to see her eyes when I give her everything—every inch, every thrust, every raw part of me. I slam in again, harder, and she *screams*, her nails digging into my back, her whole-body clenching around my cock.

"Good girl," I growl. "Fucking take it."

Her eyes roll back. Her body shakes.

And I know she's close.

I reach between us, rubbing her clit tight, fast and controlled. She gasps again, legs twitching, breath broken. Her hands slide to my face, pulling me into a kiss that's nothing but teeth and tongue and desperation.

"Come for me," I whisper into her mouth. "Right here. Right now."

She falls apart.

Hard.

She shatters around me, her walls clenching so tight it rips a sound from my throat. She cries out, one long, perfect moan as her whole body convulses against me she's wet, pulsing and shaking. Her voice breaks as she sobs my name through the peak of it.

And I fuck her through it.

Hold her together with my hands while she comes undone in them.

And I know that I'm not far behind.

She's still trembling around me, soft and wet and open in a way that tells me her body hasn't stopped feeling me yet. Her breath catches on every slow roll of my hips, her arms around my neck pulling me closer like she's not ready for it to end.

And God, neither am I.

I'm still inside her, still moving, slower now but deep so *achingly* deep with each thrust, my body trying to stretch this moment until it burns into my skin. I want her to feel every inch of me. Every flicker of what she's done to me.

She turns her face toward mine, lips brushing the corner of my mouth, her voice low and wrecked and absolutely certain. "I want to feel you come," she whispers. "*Inside me.*"

The words sink into my chest like a fuse being lit.

I grip her tighter, my hands at her waist, my forehead resting against hers, and I breathe in her sweat, her breath, her still-racing heartbeat under my lips. My next thrust is deeper, slower, and she gasps, her eyes fluttering shut like the pleasure is too much and somehow still not enough.

"You want that?" I murmur, my voice thick, breaking apart at the edges.

She nods, lips parted, and I feel her body arch into mine like it's begging.

"I want all of it," she says.

That's the end of me.

My breath shortens, my rhythm starts to falter, and I begin to move harder my body chasing that unbearable edge, that release I've been holding back like it might ruin us both. My hips snap forward again, then again, the pressure building too fast, my whole body tightening like it's winding around her.

She cups the back of my neck, her voice right at my ear, warm and steady and devastating.

"Let go," she whispers. "I want to feel you fall apart."

And I do.

I come inside her with a groan so deep it feels like it's being ripped from the center of me. My body slams forward once, twice, and then I'm lost—pulled under by heat and tightness and the rhythm of her body locking around mine. I fill her in hard, pulsing, my cock twitching as wave after wave crashes through me, intense and shaking and fucking *perfect*.

I hold onto her like I'm drowning in it, burying my face against her neck, one hand tangled in her hair, the other still gripping her hip like she might slip away if I let go too soon.

Her fingers stroke the back of my head, her other hand gliding slowly up my spine, grounding me with quiet touches as I ride it out. Her body keeps me close, keeps me inside her, keeps *all of me* even the parts I didn't mean to give.

It takes a minute for the world to return.

My heart still pounds like it's trying to climb out of my chest. My breath comes in uneven bursts. My body is spent, but I don't pull away yet. Maybe not ever.

I kiss the side of her neck. Soft. Grateful.

She turns her head just enough to meet my eyes, and there's something in her gaze, something calm and wild all at once.

"You okay?" she asks, barely a whisper.

I nod, lips ghosting against her jaw. "You just broke me in the best possible way."

And she smiles.

Not smug.

Not proud.

Just *knowing*.

Like she already knew what I'd feel. Because she felt it too.

We don't speak right away.

We just stay like that, still pressed together, her back against the wall, my body heavy against hers, both of us trying to catch our breath while the last of the fire crackles low behind us. The heat between us has shifted. It's not burning anymore.

It's *glowing*.

I kiss her shoulder, then her jaw, then her mouth slowly now, without urgency. Her lips are soft and relaxed, her arms lazy around my neck, like she's floating somewhere just below sleep.

I pull out of her gently, and she shivers as I help her with what's left of her clothes, my hands brushing her bare skin with quiet reverence. There's no rush. No need for words.

She threads her fingers through mine, and together, we walk barefoot across the stone path, back to her room. The night air is warm, humid, thick with salt and silence. Her body leans into mine, and I keep her close, protective and quiet, like we've both come through something bigger than just sex.

Inside, her room smells faintly of hibiscus and sand and sheets that still hold her shape.

We don't bother turning on the lights.

She peels off her shirt and climbs into the bed like she's done it a hundred times with me, even though this is the first. I strip down beside her, the mattress dipping beneath us, and pull her in close.

Skin to skin. Chest to her back. My arm around her waist. Her hand covering mine.

She sighs, deep and content, her breath brushing the pillow like a promise.

"You okay?" I whisper against her shoulder.

"Mmhmm," she murmurs. "Better than."

I smile, eyes heavy now, my body warm and worn and completely at peace.

The ocean murmurs beyond the windows. The fan hums. Her heartbeat slows beneath my hand.

And before long, we both drift—

not apart, not alone,

but into sleep.

Together.

Chapter 14

Piper

The light spilled into the room like liquid gold thick, warm, decadent. It painted everything it touched; the cool white walls, the tangle of sheets twisted around my legs, the worn wood of the bedside table, the delicate shadow of a palm frond trembling on the curtain. Even the air looked touched by it, sun-dusted and honey-rich, humming softly like morning had a heartbeat.

I lay still for a moment, sinking into the stillness. The bed was warm where I was, cool where he wasn't.

The pillow beside me was indented, but empty.

The scent of him lingered like clean salt, sun-warmed skin, something slightly musky and completely male. My whole body was steeped in the memory of him. Every inch of me ached in the most beautiful way. Tender. Marked. Worshipped.

I turned my head, slowly, languidly, like the morning had no reason to rush. My muscles sighed under the movement. The ache in my thighs, the soreness in my lips, the phantom sensation of his hands everywhere.

Last night hadn't just been sex.

It had been a wildfire.

A worship. A claim.

The kind of night that branded you beneath the skin.

Sunlight caught on something draped over the back of the chair by the window. His shirt a white linen, slightly wrinkled, left behind like a promise. I reached for it instinctively, pressing it to my chest, to my face. It smelled like him, like salt and smoke and something that made my lungs tighten.

Through the open window, I heard the faint sounds of morning waves brushing the shore like a sigh, distant laughter from the staff down at the beach, the rustle of a palm overhead as the breeze played in its leaves. But here, time stood still.

My room was bathed in gold.

And I bare, wrapped in memory and sun it felt like something sacred.

He had looked at me like I was holy last night.

Like I was more than a woman. Like I was an answer he hadn't known he was praying for.

And today... was the last full day.

There was a clock somewhere in this room. A suitcase that hadn't been touched. A life back home waiting like a tide I couldn't ignore forever.

But not yet.

I clutched his shirt tighter and closed my eyes for one more golden breath.

Not yet.

Eventually, I peeled myself out of bed, slipping into his shirt like it was stitched from memory. I moved through the motions, morning shower, coffee, pulling my hair back with lazy fingers but my body was still humming with him. My skin still sparkled faintly with salt; my lips still felt swollen from his kiss.

When I stepped outside, the sun was already high, casting everything in that too-perfect Caribbean glow. The kind that made every color more vivid. The sand is almost blinding. The sea was a shade of turquoise that felt impossible.

And there he was.

Jorge stood by the dive shop, his back to me, talking to one of the guests and scribbling something into the logbook. Even from here, I knew every line of that posture. The way he stood like he carried the island on his shoulders, like the weight was his and his alone. He laughed at something the guest said, and that sound reached me like a pull. Like gravity.

I didn't call his name.

I just started walking, barefoot, down the path that still held the imprint of last night.

And when he turned and saw me it was like everything else had disappeared.

We talked about the future, but neither of us knew what it held. It was careful, tentative like walking across a rope bridge in the dark. Every word felt loaded. Every silence was louder than it should've been. It was as though we were trying to imagine two lives and figure out where or if they could still collide.

Jorge sat beside me, our legs stretched out in the sand, our shoulders brushing in a rhythm more intimate than speech. The sun had climbed high, burning the waves into sheets of glass and turning every grain of sand into something too bright to look at directly. Still, we sat there, wrapped in our little bubble of shade and salt and skin.

"So," I said softly, my voice barely louder than the water behind us, "what happens next?"

I wasn't sure if I was talking about tonight. Or tomorrow. Or us.

He didn't answer right away. He didn't need to. Instead, he reached for my hand, his rough fingers finding mine like he knew they were supposed to be there all along—and held it gently, like the moment might dissolve if he squeezed too tight.

"I don't know," he said finally, his voice rough around the edges. Honest. Unapologetic.

And I loved him for it.

There was no pretending here. No future perfectly drawn with clean lines. Just two people tangled in something they couldn't name yet. Something too good to let go of and too fragile to keep without risk.

The ocean kept lapping at the shore behind us. Birds called lazily overhead. A breeze tugged at the hem of his shirt, well my shirt, technically and I closed my eyes for a second, just long enough to imagine what it would feel like to stay. To stay in this moment. This exact one. Forever.

It felt like we were dancing around a huge, unspoken question. A truth we'd both tasted but hadn't dared say aloud.

And somewhere deep inside, I could already hear it.

The music was about to stop.

And I didn't want it to.

But time didn't ask what I wanted.

Eventually, I had to go back to my room. The suitcase sat there like a stranger I didn't want to acknowledge. I packed slowly, folding things that didn't want to be folded, slipping sandals into side pockets, rolling dresses that still smelled faintly of salt and sunscreen and night.

I didn't cry. Not then. I just moved like my limbs were heavier than usual.

When I zipped the bag shut, it felt like closing a chapter I wasn't ready to stop reading.

I wheeled it to the door, pausing for one last glance. The sunlight still poured in through the curtains, golden and soft. The bed was made, but empty. The air was still.

And then I opened the door.

Jorge was there.

He stood in the corridor, hands in his pockets, eyes already on me like he'd been waiting.

"I'll take you to the airport," he said.

Just like that. No drama. No speech.

But his voice cracked a little at the end.

I nodded. And something inside me cracked too.

Not because it was ending.

But because he was still here.

He didn't reach for the suitcase. He didn't ask if I was ready. He just looked at me like I was something he hadn't figured out how to let go of yet. Like he was trying to memorize this last version of me with my hair up, lips bare, eyes brimming with something unspoken.

And I just stood there, in the doorway, torn between running into his arms and collapsing onto the floor.

The hallway smelled like ocean breeze and lemon cleaner. The world was still going on around us; people checking out, laughing in the courtyard, the distant buzz of a golf cart zipping by but for me, it had all quieted down to one man. One pair of eyes.

Jorge.

He stepped closer, not quite touching me, but near enough that I felt the heat of him, the hum of everything we weren't saying.

"I don't want this to be the end," I whispered, before I could stop myself.

He didn't answer with words. Just reached out and brushed a strand of hair behind my ear, slow and reverent. Like I was already becoming a memory.

We stood there for a moment, suspended between reality and goodbye.

Then he lifted the handle of my suitcase.

"Let's go," he said quietly.

And just like that, we started walking—toward the car, toward the airport, toward the part where I'd have to figure out how to leave someone I didn't want to be without.

The drive was mostly quiet. Not uncomfortable. Not tense. Just full.

His hand rested on the gearshift, and I kept wanting to reach out and place mine over it. But I didn't. I was afraid that if I did, I wouldn't be able to let go.

We didn't say much. We didn't need to. The silence between us was the kind that carried weight, the kind filled with everything we didn't know how to say without breaking. His thumb tapped against the wheel in rhythm with the radio. My suitcase was in the backseat. My heart is somewhere between here and nowhere.

When we reached the small island airport, everything felt too fast again. Too real. The terminal sat ahead like a deadline, and my stomach tightened the closer we got.

He parked, turned off the engine, and exhaled like it hurt. And I almost didn't want to look at him.

But I did.

And that's when he reached into the center console and pulled something out. It was a small bundle wrapped in a piece of cloth, tied with a bit of worn twine.

He pressed it into my palm gently, fingers lingering over mine.

I unfolded the fabric slowly, breath caught in my chest.

Inside was a small, carved wooden fish. It was simple, smooth, and worn from being handled. It fit in the curve of my hand like it had always been meant to be there.

The edges were sanded soft. The details of tiny scales, a perfectly imperfect tail, two eyes etched deep—were lovingly imperfect, like fingerprints in wood. Like the truth you could hold.

"I made it a few weeks ago," he said, his voice rough. "Didn't know who it was for until last night."

My chest cracked wide open.

It wasn't just a carving.

It was *him*—quiet and careful, crafted in silence, smoothed by time. It was his hands, his heart, his impossibly guarded tenderness made solid. It was the version of him he didn't let anyone else see.

And he was giving it to me.

My throat closed. My vision blurred. I tried to blink it away, but the tears came fast hot, heavy and unstoppable.

I stared down at the fish and felt the weight of it all hit me at once.

This place. This man. This version of myself I'd only just begun to recognize.

And now I had to walk away from all of it.

A single sob cracked loose, sudden and quiet, and I pressed the heel of my hand to my chest, as if I could stop my heart from unraveling right there in the passenger seat.

Jorge didn't move.

Didn't speak.

He just watched me like he didn't know whether to hold me or let me break.

"Why does this hurt so much?" I whispered.

His eyes never left mine. "Because it mattered."

I nodded, biting my lip so hard it hurt. My fingers curled around the wooden fish, holding it tight to my heart, like maybe if I squeezed hard enough, I wouldn't fall apart completely.

Outside the window, the island bustled on like nothing had changed.

But for me, everything had.

And I wasn't sure I'd ever be the same again.

My throat burned.

It wasn't expensive. It wasn't flashy. It was personal. Intimate.

It felt like a piece of him. Like something he'd carried for too long and was finally ready to give.

My vision blurred instantly, tears rising without permission. Hot, fast, unstoppable.

I clutched the fish to my chest.

And broke.

Not in a loud way. Not in a scene.

Just in the way a heart does when it knows it's been seen. Held. And is now being asked to let go.

I don't say goodbye.

Not because I don't want to.

Because I can't.

The word catches behind my teeth like it knows what it would do to me if I let it out. It's too sharp, too final. If I say it, it becomes real. If I don't, maybe this doesn't have to be the end.

So I just nod once, slowly, like I'm agreeing to something neither of us has dared name and I turn.

The carved fish is in my palm, warm from his hand, from mine. I curl my fingers around it like it's breakable, like I'm breakable, and I start walking.

Every step away from him feels like ripping something loose from my chest.

The terminal waits ahead are square, sun-washed, humming with the low buzz of people checking in, checking out, moving on. It looks like any other airport. It feels like walking into a wall.

The wind brushes my shoulders like a goodbye I didn't ask for. The sunlight wraps around me for a second longer than it should. Everything feels too alive, too beautiful, too cruel.

I keep walking.

I pass the outer doors. The air inside is colder. Sharper. Conditioned in a way that scrubs the island off your skin, like it's trying to make you forget where you've been. Who you've been.

The line is short. Just a few people ahead of me, already pulling out passports, joking about flight times, what movies they'll watch on the plane. Their voices blur. None of this feels real.

I clutch the fish tighter.

His voice is still in my head. His breath is still on my neck. My body still aches like I'm not done being touched by him.

And then something in me buckles.

I step out of line. Turn around.

The sliding doors open with a hiss, and sunlight pours in—gold and bright and blinding. I scan the curb. The walk. The edge of the lot.

His truck is still there.

But he's not in it.

The driver's side door is closed.

No shadow inside. No one leaning against the fender. No familiar shape waiting like a question mark in the sun.

I wait.

One beat. Two. Nothing.

And it hurts God, it hurts.

I tell myself he had to go. That he couldn't stay. That maybe watching me walk away would've been worse for him than it already is for me. But it doesn't help.

My lungs burn. My hand clenches around the carving like it might fuse into my skin.

I turn back toward the checkpoint, eyes stinging, throat tight.

And just as I disappear behind the corner—

Jorge steps out of the truck.

He shades his eyes with one hand, scanning the entrance like he's looking for something he's just missed. His mouth is tight. His jaw clenched. His chest rising like he's holding something in something he should have said.

But I don't see him.

And he doesn't see me.

That's how it ends.

Not with a kiss.

Not with a promise.

Just with two people looking for each other,

and never quite turning around at the same time.

And then, as I hand over my boarding pass, as the agent scans it with a polite smile, as I feel the world tilt toward leaving for good, I feel my phone buzz.

But nothing showed up on the screen.

Chapter 15

Piper

The airport hums around me, a chaotic swirl of rolling luggage, overhead announcements, and sharp-edged goodbyes. People rush by their families holding tight to sleepy children, business travelers engrossed in their phones, couples lingering in tight embraces, unwilling to let go. My grip tightens around the wooden fish in my hand, its edges smooth beneath my fingers, worn down from being held, rubbed, remembered. It's Jorge, distilled down to something I can hold onto, something that fits neatly into my palm like it's always belonged there.

But nothing about this moment feels neat.

The boarding pass in my other hand feels heavy, an anchor tugging me toward my old life, toward the safety of the familiar. Seat 22A, flight home. Home which now just feels like a place on a map, a point marked by overdue bills stacked on my kitchen counter, by an inbox filled with responsibilities that have long ceased to matter. Home a place where dreams are always shelved, stored neatly for "someday." But home doesn't have Jorge. It doesn't have mornings bathed in saltwater breezes or evenings painted with sunsets that stain the sky gold and violet, colors I never knew existed outside of paintings and dreams.

I look at the fish again, tracing its curves like it might have answers carved into its smooth surface. Stay or go. Love or safety.

A leap into the unknown or retreat to the familiar gray comfort of routine.

The weight of this decision presses hard against my ribs, squeezing my lungs until each breath comes shallow and uncertain. My heartbeat pounds louder than the airport's chaotic noise, louder than the distant roar of jet engines. This wooden fish isn't just a gift, it's an invitation, a question, a promise whispered softly beneath starlit skies. Remembering I need to turn my phone on airplane mode but before I can.

My phone buzzes again softly in my pocket, jolting me back into reality. My heart stumbles. The screen lights up, and the message is bright, brief, shattering any lingering composure:

Don't get on the plane.

Simple but the weight of those words crashes down on me.

My breath catches sharply, eyes stinging with sudden tears. Jorge's words blur my vision, transforming the crowded terminal into something distant, unreal. I can feel the intensity of his gaze even from miles away, hear the urgent plea beneath those simple words.

I'm frozen in place, pulse racing, caught in the precarious space between the life I've always known and the future I never dared to imagine. The world around me continues, oblivious to the seismic shift occurring inside my chest, while I stand there, clutching a wooden fish and an impossible choice.

Another buzz a second text, this time from an unknown number, bright and unexpected;

Don't get on the plane.

Confusion knots in my stomach, blending sharply with a surge of wild, reckless hope. My eyes dart around the terminal, heart hammering so fiercely it's hard to breathe. Who else could it be? I scan faces, desperate for a sign, for some familiar presence that might anchor me. But there's only the anonymous rush of travelers, unaware and unaffected by the turmoil tearing through me.

My thoughts spin rapidly, questions tumbling over each other in chaotic waves. Could this be fate stepping in? A cosmic nudge from the universe itself, pushing me toward a choice I've been too terrified to embrace?

My fingers tremble around my phone as I stare at those powerful, compelling words, the screen glowing with promise and possibility. My heart battles fiercely with logic, each side fighting with everything it has. The decision feels closer now, within reach but still agonizingly uncertain.

I swallow hard, gripping the wooden fish even tighter, feeling its solidity, its certainty against my palm. The choice is mine, as clear as it is overwhelming to take that step into the unknown, into a future rich with possibility, or to retreat into the comfortable yet colorless safety of what I've always known.

The noise around me fades as memories surge forward, pulling me back to last night; the gentle caress of moonlight filtering through open windows, the softness of Jorge's fingertips tracing invisible paths along my skin, his voice low and vulnerable as he shared fragments of himself, he'd kept locked away. I recall how he'd looked at me then, his eyes clear with a truth I hadn't expected but now crave more deeply than air.

In that quiet intimacy, as he whispered promises into the curve of my neck, I realized how far I had traveled but not just miles from home, but into the depths of myself. Jorge's openness had drawn out my own courage, and the woman who arrived on this island was no longer the woman standing in this airport.

I'm suddenly very clear about who I've become and who I long to be. The comfort of routine, once so appealing, now feels suffocating, like clothes that no longer fit. I want more—more than safety, more than the familiar. I crave the thrilling uncertainty that Jorge represents. The thought of stepping back into a life devoid of the colors he's shown me feels unbearable.

In a sudden rush of determination, clarity crystallizes within me. My heart pounds in decisive rhythm as I pivot sharply, moving swiftly against the current of departing travelers. Each step away from the plane feels lighter, freer, propelled by a sense of hope I haven't felt in years. I weave through clusters of people, adrenaline surging through me with every stride, eyes fixed firmly ahead, focused only on reaching Jorge.

Outside, the heat washes over me, thick and comforting, grounding me in reality. My eyes scan the bustling sidewalk, searching desperately for Jorge. Then I see him in the distance pacing nervously, hands shoved deep into his pockets, shoulders tense with worry, uncertainty etched across his features. Our eyes meet, and the relief floods his face as powerfully as it floods mine. In that instant, all uncertainty melts away, leaving only clarity.

Without a word, I rush toward him, closing the distance until I'm in his arms. His embrace is fierce, possessive, grounding, as though he fears I might vanish if he lets go. We hold each other tight, breathing in the reality of this choice we've both made, the decision to risk everything for something greater.

"I was afraid you'd gone," he whispers roughly against my hair, his voice thick with barely contained emotion.

"I couldn't," I reply, tears thickening my voice. "Not when everything I want is right here."

We pull back slightly, eyes meeting with openness and vulnerability, sharing softly spoken words filled with confessions of fears and dreams we had both kept hidden. We talk about the uncertain yet thrilling future stretching before us, acknowledging our worries, embracing our hopes, agreeing to navigate it together, step by step.

Standing hand in hand, our hearts aligned and our resolve strengthened, we turn from the airport. Together, ready to embrace whatever comes next, guided by love, courage, and the unwavering certainty of each other.

Epilogue

Piper/Jorge

P iper

The morning sunlight pours gently through the open windows of my art studio, bathing the space in warm, golden hues. Vibrant canvases, alive with colors inspired by the island's lush beauty and the ocean's endless mysteries, lean against every wall. My brushes and sketches scatter across tables, each mark a reflection of my newfound freedom and creativity.

This studio isn't just where I paint—it's my sanctuary, proof of my transformation. Every splash of paint speaks of courage, of choosing a life beyond the familiar. I smile softly, taking in the colorful chaos, feeling deeply content with how far I've come.

Jorge

The studio door creaks gently as I step inside, and my breath catches as it always does when I see Piper bathed in sunlight, absorbed in her world of colors and dreams. She glances up, eyes brightening instantly. Warmth floods my chest, powerful and steady.

"Morning," I say softly, crossing the room to wrap an arm around her waist. She leans into me easily, and my heart swells with a deep, grounding joy.

"Still creating masterpieces, I see."

She smiles, and my world tilts gently into balance. Her art, our life together—it feels seamless now, a perfect dance of independence and intimacy.

Piper

Watching Jorge in his element fills me with pride. His dive business thrives, now entwined beautifully with marine conservation and my artistic vision. Our collaboration has blossomed into something special—paintings that capture the underwater world's wonders, workshops where we teach art inspired by nature, exhibitions filled with local faces and shared laughter.

Each event feels like a shared victory, binding us closer together and to our island community. I never imagined such fulfillment, but here we are, living it fully.

Jorge

Late afternoon sun drifts lazily through the windows, painting Piper in gentle gold as she carefully sets down her brush. Her brow lifts curiously, eyes playful yet searching.

"You know," she begins, voice teasing yet cautious, "I've always wondered about that second text message."

I chuckle, knowing this conversation was inevitable. "I thought you'd ask eventually."

She tilts her head, eyes narrowed with playful suspicion. "And?"

With a rueful grin, I admit, "Lester. He borrowed my phone. He saw how torn I was and decided to intervene."

As if perfectly timed, Lester enters the studio, grinning shamelessly. "Necessary intervention. You're welcome."

Piper bursts into laughter, shaking her head affectionately. "Incorrigible."

"But effective," Lester counters cheerfully, winking as he steps out, leaving us laughing softly.

Piper

The room settles into quiet warmth once more. Jorge steps closer, gently brushing hair from my face, eyes filled with tenderness.

"We've grown so much," I whisper thoughtfully, fingers lightly tracing his jaw. "We've changed."

"We took risks," Jorge says softly, his gaze earnest, powerful. "Look at what we've created."

I smile gently, heart full of gratitude and awe. "We found balance. And each other."

Jorge

Excitement fills my chest, mirrored clearly in Piper's sparkling gaze. "We've barely begun," I murmur, voice low with the thrilling certainty of future adventures.

The world stretches before us, an endless horizon of possibility—every day a new chance, each moment alive with promise.

Piper and Jorge

The sun dips toward the horizon, painting the sky in vivid strokes of fiery orange and gentle lavender. We sit side by side on the cool sand, fingers naturally entwined, the quiet roar of waves a comforting rhythm.

Piper (POV): "This," Jorge murmurs softly, voice heavy with contentment, "this is everything I didn't know I wanted."

I rest my head against his shoulder, breathing in the familiar salt air. "Me too," I whisper, my heart swelling with peace and excitement.

Jorge (POV): We sit quietly, the simple pleasure of holding her hand anchoring me deeply in this moment. The future feels boundless, bright, and filled with Piper's radiant spirit.

Piper (POV): We gaze into the distance, the ocean vast and beautiful, the horizon infinite. Our journey has led us here, exactly where we were always meant to be—ready for whatever comes next, together, hearts wide open.

Jorge (POV): It's not an ending. It's a beautiful, thrilling beginning—ours, forever unfolding, vibrant with promise, and I can't wait to see where it leads us.

The End.

Also by

Also by Pebble James
from LPS Publishing House, LLC

Fall in love with more swoon-worthy, page-turning romance
from Pebble James—
all available on Amazon and free to read with Kindle Unlimited.

Damaged Daddy: An Age Gap Off Limits Romance
A story of forbidden love and second chances, where healing
comes from the most unexpected places.

Sweat and Desire: An Enemies to Lovers Off-Limit Romance
When sweat and sparks fly, desire is never far behind in this
steamy, heart-racing romance.

Strings of Fate: An Enemies to Lovers Contemporary Romance
Rivals on the stage, destined by fate—can love untangle the
knots of their hearts?

The Final Sale: An Off-Limits Close Proximity Romance
Scandal, redemption, and romance collide in this twisty, addictive read that will keep you guessing until the last page.

The Pitcher's Heat: An Enemies to Lovers Off-Limits Sports Romance

The only thing hotter than the summer sun is the tension between a star pitcher and the one woman who refuses to play by
his rules.

Ready for your next escape?
Find all of Pebble James' novels on Amazon—read them all with
Kindle Unlimited.

https://www.amazon.com/stores/Pebble-James/author/B0C7
WDXP87